Goosebumps®

BAD HARE DAY

R.L. STINE

AN
APPLE
PAPERBACK

SCHOLASTIC INC.
New York Toronto London Auckland Sydney

A PARACHUTE PRESS BOOK

ISBN 0-590-56878-7

12 11 10 9 8 7 6 5 4 3 2   6 7 8 9/9 0 1/0

Printed in the U.S.A.   40

First Scholastic printing, March 1996

1

"Pick a card, any card." I spread out the deck of cards in front of Sue Mailer, facedown. She giggled and picked one.

"Don't show it to me," I warned her. She glanced at the card, keeping it hidden from me.

A small crowd of kids gathered on the school steps to watch. School was out for the day. Sue showed them her card.

I love doing magic tricks — especially in front of an audience. My dream is to be a great magician like my idol, Amaz-O.

I've been playing around with stage names. My real name is Tim Swanson — but that's way too boring for a professional magician. I've been thinking of calling myself Swanz-O. My best friend, Foz, thinks Swanz-O sounds like a laundry detergent.

"Now, Sue," I said in a louder voice, so everybody could hear me. "Put the card back in the deck."

1

Sue slipped the card in with the others. I shuffled the deck and tapped it three times. "I will now make your card rise to the top of the deck," I announced.

Tap, tap, tap. I picked up the top card and showed it to Sue. "Was this your card?" I asked her.

Her eyebrows shot up in amazement. "The three of clubs!" she cried. "That was my card!"

"How'd you do that?" Jesse Brown asked.

"Magicians never reveal their secrets," I said, bowing. "And now, for my next trick — "

"I know how he did it." My little sister, Ginny, suddenly popped up in the crowd. The sound of her scratchy voice made my hair stand on end. She loves to spoil my magic shows.

But a true magician doesn't let anything throw him. I grinned my biggest, fakest grin at the little brat.

"Ladies and gentlemen, my lovely assistant, Ginny!"

"I'm not your assistant, freak-face," Ginny snarled. "You won't catch me doing nerdy magic tricks. I'm into karate. Hi-ya!" She demonstrated her karate chop.

Some of the kids laughed. I pretended to laugh, too. "Ha, ha. Isn't she a riot?"

Everybody says Ginny looks like an angel. She has long, wavy blond hair, rosy cheeks, big blue eyes. People always ooh and aah over her.

2

No one ever oohs and aahs over me. I've got curly light-brown hair and hazel eyes. I'm twelve, which Mom says isn't a "cute age."

My nose is long and curves up at the end like a hot dog. Ginny likes to flick the end of my nose with her finger and say, "Boi-oi-oing."

Her nose is small and perfect, of course.

I tried to continue my show, Ginny or no Ginny. I slipped the deck of cards into my pocket and yanked out my magic scarf. "Now, be amazed as I — "

Ginny reached into my pocket and snatched out the cards. "Look, everybody!" she cried, showing them the cards. "*All* the cards are the three of clubs!"

Ginny started passing the cards around so everyone could see.

"Hey! Give those back!" I protested. I grabbed the cards away. It was true. Every single card in the deck was the three of clubs. But no one was supposed to know that.

"You're a phony," Sue mumbled.

"No — wait!" I cried. "Watch this!"

I whipped out my magic rings — two large silver hoops hooked together. The kids quieted down a little.

"These silver rings are locked together," I declared. "They're completely solid — linked together forever!" I tugged on them to show that they wouldn't come apart.

3

Then I handed them to Jesse. "Try to pull the rings apart," I told him. He pulled hard. He pulled lightly. He pulled hard again. He jangled them around. The rings stayed hooked together.

I took them back. "The rings will never come apart," I said. "Unless I say the magic words." I waved one hand over the rings. "Hocus pocus!" I gently pulled the rings apart. A couple of kids clapped.

"You're not going to fall for *that* old trick, are you?" Ginny mocked. "You want to know how he does it?" She grabbed the rings away and began to demonstrate. "They're trick rings — "

"I will now make my lovely assistant disappear!" I cried, shoving Ginny aside. "Beat it!"

"Stop pushing me!" she shouted. "Hi-ya!"

She karate-kicked me in the stomach.

"Oof!" I doubled over. Everybody laughed and clapped.

"That's a great trick!" Sue said.

I clutched my stomach. Some trick.

Stupid Ginny and her karate kicks. Why did Mom have to take her to that martial-arts school? My life has been miserable ever since. She's only ten, and she fights way better than I do. I've got the bruises to show it.

"Kick him again!" somebody yelled.

Ginny crouched, ready to attack.

"Try it, and I'll tell Mom where that dent in the refrigerator door came from," I warned her.

She backed off. She knew Mom would kill her for karate-chopping the fridge just because we were out of ice cream.

"She's not going to kick him," Jesse said. "Show's over."

The kids drifted away.

"Wait!" I cried. "Come back!"

"See you tomorrow, Tim," Sue said. Everybody began to head for home.

"Thanks for wrecking everything, Ginny," I snapped.

She flicked my nose. "Boi-oi-oing."

"Stop it!" I swatted her away. "You're definitely going to get it. I'm telling Mom about the fridge for sure."

"Go ahead," she taunted. "But if you do, I'll give you the freezer chop." She waved her arms through the air, making those weird karate noises. "*Wah wah wee — ah!* Right to the neck. You'll never walk again!"

She trotted away. "See you at home, Swanz-O!"

This is what I have to deal with every day of my life. A little sister who could kill me if she wanted to. What can I do? I'm helpless against her.

That's one reason I want to be a magician. Maybe Ginny can karate-chop my arms off — but not if I make her disappear first!

I sighed and buttoned up my denim jacket. It

was almost four o'clock and getting chilly. The wind had picked up, too. When is it going to get warm? I wondered. It's the end of March — it's supposed to be spring already.

The school door burst open. "I'm outta here!" Foz shouted.

Foz's real name is Foster Martin. But he doesn't look like a Foster. He's a Foz. He's chubby, with a brown buzz cut. His shirt is always untucked.

"Where've you been?" I asked him.

"Mrs. Pratt made me stay after school," he replied, making a disgusted face.

"Why?" I asked.

"No reason," Foz said.

Foz has to stay after school almost every day. He always says it's for no reason.

I picked up my magic kit and started down the school steps. Foz followed. We left the school grounds and walked toward town.

"What were *you* doing at school so late?" he asked.

"I was trying out a few magic tricks. Ginny told everybody how they work. It was a disaster."

"You need better tricks," Foz said. "Lots of kids have the same magic kit as yours."

"You're right," I agreed, rattling my kit. "This is amateur stuff. I'm ready for some *real* magic tricks. Professional ones."

"Like a hat you can pull a rabbit out of."

"Or that spinning box Amaz-O has," I added.

6

Amaz-O was my hero — the greatest magician ever. "Did you see him on TV last week? His assistant stepped into a big black box. Amaz-O spun it around three times, and she disappeared!"

"He's doing a show at Midnight Mansion," Foz said. Midnight Mansion is a club in town where magicians perform every night.

"I know. I wish I could go. But the tickets cost twenty-five dollars."

We turned onto Bank Street and headed toward the center of town. It wasn't on the way home, but Foz knew what I was doing. Malik's Magic Shoppe was on Bank Street. I stopped in there at least once a week, just to drool over the cool tricks they had.

"Malik's has a bunch of new tricks," I told Foz. "Designed by Amaz-O himself."

"I'll bet they're expensive," Foz said.

"They are." I reached into my pocket to see how much money I had. Five bucks.

"That'll buy you a squirting flower," Foz said. "Maybe."

I stuffed the bill back into my pocket. "You've got to see this stuff, anyway. There's a table — you put a plate or something on it — it can be anything you want. The plate will rise up over the table and float!"

"How does it work?" Foz asked.

"I don't know. Mr. Malik wouldn't tell me. He said you have to buy the trick to find out."

7

"How much does it cost?"

"Five hundred dollars."

Foz rolled his eyes. "I guess you'll have to stick with card tricks."

"I guess." I sighed.

A little bell rang as we opened the door to Malik's. I breathed in the musty smell of the shop. It was jam-packed with old tricks, new tricks, magic books, and costumes. There were even cages in the back for rabbits and doves. Mr. Malik sold everything.

I called out, "Hi, Mr. Malik." He stood behind the cash register. He was a short, bald old man with a fat stomach.

I waited for Mr. Malik to say, "What's new, Magoo?" in his gravelly voice. That's how he greets all his regular customers.

I called out, "Hi!" again, but he didn't answer. He just stood there and grunted.

"Mr. Malik?" Foz and I crept closer to the counter.

"Unh!" Mr. Malik grunted. He stumbled forward.

Something was sticking out of his stomach. A sword!

"Mr. Malik?" I asked. "Are you okay?"

He clutched the handle of the sword and moaned in pain.

Someone had stabbed him!

"Help me!" he groaned. "Please — help!"

Foz and I froze in fear. I let out a gasp — but I was too frightened to move. Foz's whole body trembled.

Mr. Malik uttered another groan. Then his expression changed. He pulled out the sword — and he tossed it to me.

"Hey!" I cried. "It's a fake!"

Mr. Malik laughed. He rubbed his round stomach, which hadn't been stabbed at all. "What's new, Magoo?" he chuckled. "Get a load of that trick sword. Just got it in today."

I tested the sword against my own stomach. It had a sliding blade. I pushed the blade into the handle, then let go. It popped out again. Very cool.

Foz fingered the blade. "Think of the tricks you could play on Ginny with a sword like this!"

"Like it, Tim?" Mr. Malik asked. "Only twenty bucks."

I shook my head. "We're just looking, Mr. Malik."

He hung the sword on the wall behind him. "All right. Take your time and look around. But would it kill you to actually *buy* something once in a while?"

Mr. Malik always said that, too.

I wandered to the back of the shop. I checked out a rack of magician's jackets. I pulled a sparkly blue tuxedo jacket off the rack and tried it on. It had a trick sleeve for hiding things.

9

I stared at myself in the mirror. I pretended to announce myself. "The Amazing Swanz-O!"

Foz shook his head in disgust. "That name is so lame."

"Yeah, you're right." I thought of another name. "How about 'Swanson the Magnificent'?"

"It's okay," Foz said. "A little boring, but okay."

He tried on a top hat and added, "You need something cooler, like 'Tim the Destroyer.' "

"That sounds like a wrestler," I commented.

"At least it's not wimpy," Foz retorted. "Like Swanz-O."

"Hey, boys." Mr. Malik shuffled toward us. He held out two tickets.

"Take these, if you want them," he said. "Two free passes to Amaz-O's magic show tomorrow night."

"Wow!" I cried. I took a ticket and read it.

ADMIT ONE
AN EVENING OF MAGIC WITH THE
GREAT AMAZ-O
MARCH 23
10 P.M.
MIDNIGHT MANSION

"Thanks Mr. Malik! I can't believe we'll get to see Amaz-O in person!" I gushed. "Tomorrow night!"

"Tomorrow night?" Foz frowned at his ticket. "I can't go. My aunt and uncle are coming over. It's my mother's birthday."

"So? This is a once-in-a-lifetime chance! Your mother has a birthday every year."

Foz stuffed the ticket into my palm, shaking his head. "I know my mom — and she won't see it that way. Anyway, tomorrow night is a school night."

I'd forgotten about that. I hoped my mom would let *me* go. Ten o'clock was pretty late to go out on a school night.

She has to let me go, I decided. She just *has* to. What kind of horrible mother would keep her son from seeing his hero in person? Only a really mean, monstery mother.

My mother is a grump, but she's not a monster.

I took off the blue jacket and hung it back up on the rack. A large wooden box caught my eye. It was the size of a coffin, brightly painted with red and yellow stars. I lifted the lid.

The box was empty, lined with blue velvet on the inside. "What's the box do, Mr. Malik?" I asked.

"That's for sawing people in half," Mr. Malik replied.

I examined the inside of the box, trying to figure out how it worked. I found no secret compartments or panels or anything.

"How does it work?" I asked Mr. Malik.

11

"You going to buy it?" he demanded.

"Well — how much does it cost?"

"Two-fifty."

"Two dollars and fifty cents? I can afford that."

Mr. Malik waved me away and started toward the stockroom at the back of the shop. "Two dollars and fifty cents," he muttered. "In your dreams."

"He meant two *hundred* and fifty dollars, Brainz-O," Foz said.

I tried to cover myself. "I knew that. I was joking."

Foz fiddled with a cool-looking trick in the corner. I moved closer to see.

"It's a guillotine," Foz said. "For chopping off heads."

The guillotine had a place for the victim to rest his head at the bottom — and a razor-sharp blade at the top.

Mr. Malik emerged from the back room. "I'm closing up soon, boys," he called.

"I just want to see how this works," Foz said. He twisted a lever on the guillotine.

"Foz — no!" I cried.

The blade slid down the guillotine.

And landed with a horrifying *thunk*.

"My hand!" Foz shrieked. "My hand!"

2

Mr. Malik gasped. "I'll call an ambulance! Nine-one-one!" He grabbed the phone.

The guillotine blade had sliced right through Foz's hand. He screamed in pain.

"Oh!" Foz moaned. "I cut off my hand!" he wailed. "I'll never write again!"

I started laughing.

"Why are you laughing?" Mr. Malik demanded. "This is an emergency!"

"No, it's not." Foz held up his hands to show that he was fine. "Got a paper towel? I need to wipe off this fake blood."

"Fake?" Mr. Malik stammered. "Fake blood?"

"We got you back for that sword trick," I told him.

Mr. Malik clutched his sweaty forehead in his hands. "I'm so stupid! I know that's a trick guillotine. Why did I fall for such a dumb joke?"

"Hey," Foz protested. "It was a lot funnier than your sword-in-the-stomach joke."

Mr. Malik wiped his brow and smiled. "All right, boys. Enough tricks. It's five o'clock. Get out of here." He shoved us toward the door.

"Thanks for the tickets, Mr. Malik," I called. "See you next week."

"Sure. Next week, when I'll have a new shipment of magic tricks you won't buy."

The bell on the door jangled as we left the shop. Foz and I walked down Bank Street toward home.

"Sure you won't go to Midnight Mansion tomorrow night?" I asked him.

"I can't. Your mom will never let you go, either."

"I'll find a way," I insisted. "You'll see."

We paused in front of Foz's house. "Come over to my house after school tomorrow," I said. "I'm giving another magic show. Only this time Ginny won't wreck it."

"I'll be there," Foz promised.

"And bring your sister's rabbit," I added.

Foz shuffled his feet uncomfortably. "Clare is not going to like that . . ." he began.

"Please, Foz," I begged. "I'm going to finish building my rabbit table tonight. The rabbit trick is going to be so amazing — "

"I'll try to bring the rabbit," Foz said. "But if anything happens to it, Clare will kill me."

"Nothing will happen to it — I promise."

I waved good-bye to Foz and went home. "The

Great Swanzini is here!" I announced as I burst into the kitchen.

"You mean the Great Jerk," Ginny mumbled. She sat at the kitchen table, folding napkins. She reached up and flicked at my nose. "Boi-oi-oing."

"Get off me." I slapped her hand away.

Mom set a plate of chicken on the table. "Go wash up, Tim," she ordered. "And tell your father supper is ready."

"Look, Mom." I held up a quarter. Then, with a flick of my wrist, I slipped it up my sleeve. "I made the quarter disappear!"

I showed her my two empty hands.

"Very nice. I see two hands that haven't been washed yet," Mom said impatiently.

"I saw the quarter go up your sleeve," Ginny sneered.

"No one appreciates me around here," I complained. "Someday I'm going to be the greatest magician in the world. And my own family doesn't care!"

Mom strode to the kitchen door. "Bill!" she called upstairs to my dad. "Supper!"

I made my way out of the kitchen to wash my hands. My parents didn't take my magic act seriously. They thought it was just a hobby.

But Ginny's karate lessons were the most important thing in the world, of course. Mom always said, "Girls need to know how to defend them-

15

selves." Now I needed to defend myself against my own sister!

I returned to the kitchen and sat down. Mom plunked a piece of chicken down beside the rice on my plate. Dad and Ginny were already eating.

"I had a terrible day at work today," Mom grumbled, ripping into her chicken. She's a high school guidance counselor. "First Michael Lamb threatened to beat up another boy. His teacher yelled at him, and he threatened to beat her up, too. She sent him to my office. When I tried to talk to him, he said he'd beat *me* up. So I called his mother in — and *she* tried to beat me up. I had to call the police!"

"That's a piece of cake next to *my* day," Dad complained. Dad sells cars. "Some guy came in and said he wanted to test-drive the new minivan. I handed him the keys, and he took off. He never came back. He stole the car!"

I sighed and shoveled rice into my mouth. Dinner is like this every night. Both of my parents hate their jobs.

"I had a really tough day, too," Ginny put in. "Michael Franklin teased me. So I had to karate-kick him in the leg!"

I smirked. "Poor you."

Mom's forehead wrinkled — her concerned look. "You didn't hurt yourself, did you, Ginny?"

"No," Ginny replied. "But I *could* have."

"What about me?" I protested. "*I'm* the one who got kicked in the stomach. And it hurt a lot!"

"You seem to be fine now," Dad chimed in.

I gave up. I knew that arguing would get me nowhere. Mom and Dad always take Ginny's side.

"Is there any dessert?" Ginny demanded.

"Ice cream," Mom answered.

"I'll clear the table," I offered, hoping it would put Mom in a better mood. I needed both Mom and Dad to be in a good mood.

Because I was about to ask the big question.

Would they let me go to Midnight Mansion tomorrow night?

Would they?

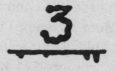

3

I stood up, collecting dirty plates. "Guess what? Amaz-O is doing his act at Midnight Mansion tomorrow night. Mr. Malik gave me two free passes." I held my breath, waiting for their answer.

"Excellent!" Ginny cried. "That means I can go too!"

"I'm not taking you," I told her. "I'll ask Mark or Jesse or somebody. Anybody but you." I dropped the plates in the sink. They crashed but didn't break.

"Careful, Tim," Mom warned.

Ginny slithered over to the sink and tried to hug me. "Please, Tim. I'm your sister. Your only sister in the whole world. I'd do *anything* for you. You have to take me with you!"

"Neither one of you is going," Dad said quietly. "It's a school night."

"But Dad, it's free!" I protested. "Just this

18

once. Amaz-O is my hero. I'll never get another chance to see him in person!"

"What time does the show start?" Mom asked.

"Ten o'clock," I told her.

She shook her head. "Absolutely not. You're not going out at ten o'clock on a school night. Especially not to a nightclub. You're much too young." She furiously spooned ice cream into a bowl.

"Mom — please!" I begged. "I'm twelve. I can handle it."

"You heard your mother," Dad said. "You'll have other chances to see Amaz-O, Tim. Don't worry."

Mom offered me a bowl of ice cream. "I don't want it," I grumbled. I stormed out of the kitchen. As I left, I heard Ginny say, "Good. Now I'll get two bowls of ice cream."

Stupid Ginny, I thought. Stupid Mom and stupid Dad. My one chance to see my idol, the great Amaz-O — and they won't let me go.

I wandered into the garage. In the corner stood a new trick I was building — the rabbit table. It was a square table that came up to my waist. The top had a hole in it that led to a secret compartment under the table.

I planned to hide a rabbit in the compartment and cover the hole with my magic top hat. When I pressed a pedal at the foot of the table, the bottom of the secret compartment would rise up. Then I'd lift my hat — and there would be the rabbit!

The table was almost finished. I turned it upside down and hammered on the bottom of the secret compartment.

This trick is going to knock everybody out tomorrow afternoon, I thought. I'll be almost as amazing as Amaz-O!

I was so busy hammering I didn't hear the garage door open. Two baby blue high-tops suddenly appeared in front of me. I didn't have to look up. I knew Ginny's smelly sneakers when I saw them.

"Go away," I commanded.

She never listens to me. "You going to do the rabbit trick tomorrow?" she asked.

"Uh-huh. Now go away."

"Where are you going to get the rabbit?"

I set down my hammer. "I'm going to turn *you* into a rabbit."

"Ha ha." She flipped her wavy blond hair. "You know what this table would be perfect for?" she asked. "Karate-chopping. I'll bet I could chop it in half with one hand."

"Try it and I'll — "

"You'll what?" she taunted.

What could I do to her? Not much. "I'll turn you into a rabbit for *real*," I threatened.

"Oh, yeah? How are you going to do that?"

"It's easy," I replied. "Mr. Malik showed me

how. Tonight, while you're sleeping, I'm going to sneak into your room and turn you into a rabbit."

"Give me a break," Ginny said. "That is so dumb."

"Maybe. Maybe not. I guess we'll find out tonight." I picked up my hammer again. "I hope you like carrots," I told her.

"You're crazy," she said. She hurried out of the garage.

Well, I thought. At least that got rid of her for a while.

I set the table on its legs again. All I had to do was paint it, and it would be ready.

Wouldn't it be great? I thought as I opened a can of blue paint. Wouldn't it be great if I really *could* turn Ginny into a rabbit?

But that was impossible. Wasn't it?

4

"We want the rabbit trick! We want the rabbit trick!"

Ginny sat in the grass in our backyard. Six or seven other kids sat around. I was in the middle of my magic act. Ginny was stirring up trouble.

She knew I didn't have a rabbit for the trick. I was still waiting for Foz to show up.

Where is he? I wondered. He's ruining my show!

The other kids joined in Ginny's chant. "The rabbit trick! The rabbit trick!"

I tried to stall them. "The amazing, incredible rabbit trick is coming up," I promised. "But first — wouldn't you like to see me pull a quarter out of Ginny's ear again?"

"No!" the kids yelled. "Boo!"

"Karate fight!" Sue called. "We want a karate fight. Ginny versus Tim!"

Things were getting ugly.

At last I glimpsed Foz at the side of the house. He waved at me frantically.

"Intermission!" I announced. "I'll be back in two minutes. And then — I'll pull a rabbit out of my hat!"

I hurried over to Foz. A big cardboard box sat at his feet.

"What took you so long?" I demanded.

"I'm sorry," Foz said. "I almost had to rip the rabbit out of Clare's hands."

I opened the box. Clare's big white rabbit lifted its nose and sniffed at me. I grabbed it and stuffed it under my jacket.

"Be careful!" Foz warned. "If anything happens to it, my sister will chop me into rabbit food!"

"The rabbit will be fine," I told him. "What could happen to it?"

I sneaked the rabbit to the table. With my back to the audience, I stuffed it into the secret compartment and plopped my hat on top.

Then I turned to face the kids. None of them had seen the rabbit. Perfect.

"Ladies and gentlemen!" I called. "Thanks for being so patient. Here is the moment you've all been waiting for — "

"Karate fight!" Ginny called.

"Even better than a karate fight!" I said. "I, the Great Timothini, will now pull a rabbit out of my hat!"

Ginny snorted. "The Great Timothini?"

I pointed at her. "You, in the front row. Quiet!"

"You be quiet!" Ginny shot back.

"Get on with it!" Jesse called.

"Okay. I need complete silence now. I must concentrate."

To my surprise, the kids actually quieted down. Even Ginny. Everyone stared up at me, waiting.

I lifted my hat off the table. "As you can see, my hat is empty. It's an ordinary, everyday top hat. Sue, will you please examine the hat?"

I passed the hat to Sue. She turned it over. "It looks like a regular hat to me," she declared.

I set the hat on the table, covering the secret compartment. "Thank you, Sue. Now — watch carefully."

I waved my arms over the hat. "Abracadabra, abracadeer, rabbit, rabbit, rabbit — *appear!*"

I stepped on the pedal to make the rabbit rise up. Then I lifted the hat with a flourish.

Nothing there. The hat stood empty.

I checked the secret compartment. No rabbit there, either.

My heart pounded. How could this be?

"The rabbit!" I cried. "It's gone!"

5

What have I done? I thought in horror.

My trick must have worked better than I thought!

I glanced up and saw Ginny pointing across the backyard. "There it goes!" she cried. "There's the rabbit!"

I whirled around. Clare's white rabbit was hopping away.

How could that happen? I wondered. I glanced into the secret compartment again.

I'd left one side of the secret compartment open. How could I have been so stupid?

"Tim — you promised!" Foz screamed. "Grab it!"

I chased after the rabbit. Foz huffed behind me. The rabbit had already hopped halfway across our next-door neighbors' backyard. I glanced back. Ginny and the other kids were yelling and running after us.

The rabbit stopped behind a bush. I sped up —
and pounced.

"Got him!" I cried. But the rabbit slipped out
of my hands and bounded away.

"He's headed for the stream!" Ginny shouted.

A muddy stream ran behind all the backyards
on our block. The rabbit disappeared behind the
trees that hid the stream.

Whooping like crazy, Ginny led the kids after
the rabbit.

"Stop!" I yelled. "You're scaring it away!"

But none of them listened to me. There was
nothing to do but keep chasing.

"Don't let the rabbit hop into the water!" Foz
screamed. "He'll drown!"

"He won't drown," I told Foz. "That stream is
only about two inches deep."

"Just catch the rabbit!" Foz ordered. He was
in a total panic. Maybe his sister really *would* chop
him into rabbit food.

The rabbit hopped through the mud and across
the stream into the Darbys' yard. I shoved the
other kids aside. I splashed through the stream.

The rabbit stopped. Its ears twitched.

I motioned to the others to keep still. I squatted
down and crept toward the rabbit.

I saw why it had stopped. The Darbys' cat, Boo
Boo, crouched low in the grass, waiting to pounce.

The rabbit was trapped between us. I crawled
closer. Closer. I was almost there. . . .

"Watch out for the cat!" Foz shrieked.

With a yowl, the cat leaped. The rabbit bounced about a foot in the air, I missed him.

Everybody raced after him again. I threw Foz a dirty look.

"You're ruining everything!" I shouted.

"*You're* the one who lost him in the first place!" Foz yelled back.

"Hey!" Sue called. "Look at Ginny!"

Ginny had raced to the head of the pack. The rabbit paused, then started running again. Ginny took a flying leap. "*Yaw, hee ha how!*" she screeched in her weirdo karate voice.

She landed on her feet in front of the rabbit. It tried to change course. Too late.

"Hiii — ya!" Ginny swooped down and grabbed the rabbit. She held him over her head like a trophy.

"I got him!" she cried. "I got him!"

"Yay, Ginny!" Everyone crowded around her, slapping her on the back.

"Don't let him go!" Foz cried. He hurried over to Ginny and snatched the rabbit away.

We all started back to my yard. "Awesome trick, Tim." Jesse patted me on the back. "You almost made the rabbit really disappear!"

Everybody laughed. "You should change your stage name, Timothini," Sue chimed in. "How about 'The Great Goofballini'?"

"Or 'Mess-Up the Magnificent'!" Jesse suggested.

I sighed and shut my eyes. Another magic show — another disaster.

"I can't believe you almost lost my sister's rabbit," Foz grumbled.

"I'm sorry, Foz. I'll be more careful next time."

He clutched the rabbit tightly to his chest. "Next time, get your own rabbit."

He hurried to the side of the house and stuffed the rabbit into the box.

"Anybody want to come over to my house?" Jesse called. He lived next door. "I've got a great trick to show you — the disappearing dog. I let go of his leash, and he runs away!"

Laughing, the other kids drifted over to Jesse's house. Foz took the rabbit home to his sister.

"You going over to Jesse's?" Ginny asked.

I shook my head. "I'm going inside for a snack."

"Maybe you should do your magic act inside from now on," Ginny said. "Then your tricks won't be able to escape from you!" She giggled.

"Very funny," I mumbled. "You won't be laughing so hard when I turn *you* into a rabbit. I don't think rabbits know how to laugh."

"Ooh. I'm scared." She rolled her eyes.

"You'd better be." I leaned close to her and whispered. "Tonight's the night. Tonight, while you're sleeping, I'll turn you into a rabbit. And if you try to run away, the Darbys' cat will get you."

She rolled her eyes again. Then she reached up to tweak my nose. "Boi-oi-oing."

28

She trotted off to Jesse's house.

I definitely need better magic tricks, I thought as I dragged myself into the house. Better equipment, too. So I can do really *cool* tricks. Tricks that actually work.

I thought of all the stuff Mr. Malik sold in his shop. If I could have just one of those tricks, I could do a great act. I've got to get one somehow.

But how?

That night everybody went to bed early. Mom and Dad were exhausted and crabby after another bad day at work.

"Today was the worst day ever!" Mom grumbled. "I'm so exhausted. Everybody to bed!"

Ginny and I knew better than to protest. We didn't want to stay up, anyway, with Mom and Dad grouching around all evening.

I lay in bed with the lights off, trying to sleep. Amaz-O's show is tonight, I thought miserably. He's performing tonight, only a few miles away from my house. I have free passes. And I can't go. It's not fair!

How am I ever going to be a great magician if I never see any magic shows? Amaz-O is the greatest of the great — and I have to miss my one chance to see him!

Or do I? A wicked thought popped into my head. Why *should* I miss the show?

I've got the tickets. I can ride to Midnight Mansion on my bike. I could sneak out of the house for a couple of hours — and Mom and Dad would never have to know.

I rolled over in bed and peered at my alarm clock. The dial glowed in the dark. Nine-forty.

The show would start in twenty minutes, I knew. I could still make it if I left right now.

I couldn't stand to think about it any longer. I had to go.

I slid out of bed, hoping my mattress wouldn't creak. I tiptoed across the room to my dresser. I silently pulled on a pair of jeans and a shirt.

Sneakers in hand, I carefully opened my bedroom door. The house was dark. I heard Dad snoring in my parents' room down the hall.

I crept toward the stairs. Am I really doing this? I thought, suddenly nervous. Am I really sneaking out in the middle of the night to go to Midnight Mansion?

6

Yes — I'm really doing it, I thought. I'll do *anything* to see Amaz-O. It's totally worth the risk.

What's the worst that could happen?

Mom and Dad could find out. Then what? Maybe they'd ground me. But I will have seen the great Amaz-O in person. And while I'm grounded, I can try to learn some of Amaz-O's tricks.

Anyway, I won't get caught. I won't.

I paused at the top of the stairs. The stairs in my house are the creakiest stairs in the universe.

Once when I was little, I tried to sneak downstairs on Christmas Eve to see what Santa had left me. I barely touched the top step with my foot — *CRRREEEEAAAK!* Mom burst out of her room before I even had a chance to try the second step.

It's not going to happen this time, I told myself. I'll take each step very slowly. I'll lean on the banister to keep them from creaking. No one will wake up. No one will hear me.

I put both my hands on the banister and rested my weight on it. Then I set my right foot carefully — the toe, then the heel — on the top step.

Crick. Just a tiny little sound. I'm sure no one heard it, I thought.

I shifted my hands down the banister and took another step. This one made no creak at all.

So far, so good.

I took the third step. *Creak.* Not a rip-roaring loud creak, but louder than the first. I froze.

I listened for the sound of someone stirring in the house.

Silence. All clear.

If Amaz-O only knew what I'm going through to see him, I thought. I must be his biggest fan on the face of the earth.

I made it all the way down the stairs with only one more creak. I breathed a sigh of relief.

I'm safe now, I thought. I'll wait until I get outside to put my shoes on. Then I'll grab my bike and go.

I tiptoed across the cold hallway floor. I reached for the handle of the front door. Twisted it.

Almost there.

Almost.

Then a shrill voice demanded, "Tim — where do you think you're going?"

7

I spun around. Ginny!

She was dressed in jeans and a sweater, all ready to go out. She bounded down the stairs.

"Ssshhhhhhhh! You'll wake up Mom and Dad!"

I grabbed her by the arm and yanked her out the front door.

"What are you doing up?" I demanded.

"I was waiting for you to come into my room and turn me into a rabbit," she replied. "Or pretend to, anyway."

"I'm not going to do that tonight," I said. "Go back to bed."

"What are *you* doing up? Where are you going?"

I sat on the front steps and pulled on my sneakers. "Out to the garage," I lied. "To practice a new trick."

"You are not. I know where you're going. To Midnight Mansion!"

I grabbed her by the shoulders. "Okay. You're

33

right. I'm going to Midnight Mansion. Don't tell Mom and Dad — promise?"

"I want to go!" she insisted. "Let me go with you."

"No. Go back to bed — and don't tell. Or you'll be sorry."

"You *have* to take me!" she declared. "If you don't, I'll run upstairs and tell Mom and Dad right now. Then you'll never get to see Amaz-O."

"You wouldn't."

"I would."

I knew she would.

"All right," I agreed. "You can come. But you have to be good and do everything I tell you to do."

"Maybe I will — and maybe I won't."

I sighed. I had to take her, no matter how bratty she was. If I did, she'd never tell — because then she'd be in as much trouble as me.

"Let's go," I whispered.

We sneaked into the garage and got our bikes. Then we pedaled off into the night.

It felt strange riding down Bank Street late at night. The shops were all closed and dark. Hardly any traffic on the street.

Oh, no. A police car up ahead — cruising toward us down Bank Street. If he spotted us, he'd stop us for sure. And then he'd take us home. And then we'd *really* be in trouble.

I searched desperately for a place to hide. The police couldn't miss us — Bank Street was lined with streetlights.

"Ginny!" I called. "Quick — out of the light!" I swerved into the dark doorway of a dress shop. Ginny followed. We leaped off our bikes and pressed ourselves into the shadows.

The police car glided past. I held my breath as the headlights brushed across us. The car stopped.

"He saw us!" Ginny whispered. "Run!"

I grabbed her arm to stop her. "Wait." I peeked out into the street.

The police car was idling, but the driver stayed inside.

"It's a red light," I told Ginny. A few seconds later the light turned green, and the police car rolled away.

"We're safe now," I said. We hopped back onto our bikes and rode off.

Midnight Mansion loomed huge and dark at the edge of town. People said that a crazy old woman had lived alone in the mansion for forty years. She was rich, but so stingy she wore ragged old clothes and ate nothing but peanut butter, right out of the jar.

When people tried to visit her, she screamed, "Go away!" and threw rocks at them. She had about fifty cats. When she died, a businessman bought the mansion and turned it into a nightclub.

I braked in front of the old house and stared at it. Midnight Mansion.

It looked like a spooky old castle made of sooty black stone. Three stories tall, with two towers shooting up into the night sky. Vines crept across the roof. A floodlight threw creepy shadows over the house.

I'd seen the mansion a million times before. But late at night it looked bigger and darker than usual. I thought I saw bats fluttering around the two towers.

"No wonder the old lady went crazy," Ginny whispered. "Living in a spooky place like that."

"Do you think she kept prisoners in those towers?" I wondered.

"I think she had a torture chamber in the basement," Ginny said.

We walked our bikes up to the entrance. People hurried inside to see Amaz-O's magic show. Three men in long black capes breezed past us. A woman with long black hair, black lipstick, and pointy black fingernails smiled at me.

"Where did all these weird people come from?" Ginny asked.

I shrugged. "Let's go in. The show is about to start."

We locked our bikes and ran up the long stone steps. We entered a big hall lit by a crystal chandelier. We crossed the hall to a doorway covered by a heavy red curtain.

A tall, thin man in a black tuxedo guarded the curtain. He reached out a long, bony finger to stop us.

He had no hair, a pencil neck, and dark, hollow eye sockets. "He looks like a skeleton," Ginny whispered to me.

I pulled the two tickets out of my back pocket and handed them to him.

"Very good," he croaked in a low voice. "But where are your parents? I can't seat children without their parents."

My parents? Think fast, Swanz-O, I told myself. "Um — my parents. Yes. Well, my parents, you see . . ." I had a feeling he didn't want to hear that my parents were home sleeping.

"They're outside, parking the car," I lied. "They'll be here in a minute. They told us to come in and get a table."

The man's hollow black eyes seemed to burn a hole in my brain. Would he buy it?

"I don't like it. But all right." He led us through the red curtain. The houselights went down just as we walked in. He showed us to a table right next to the stage.

"Excellent!" I said to Ginny as we sat down. "The best seats in the whole place!"

"This is so exciting!" she exclaimed. "I can't

believe we're in a real, grown-up nightclub. By ourselves!"

The eerie-looking host stood by the red curtain, watching us. "We may not be here long," I warned her. "That skeleton guy's got his eye on us. When he realizes we're not here with our parents — "

"Shh! The show's starting."

A voice came over a loudspeaker. "Ladies and gentlemen! Midnight Mansion is proud to present the most famous magician in America. The fabulous, the incredible, the mind-boggling Amaz-O!"

A drum roll, and then horns bleating "Ta da!" The audience clapped and cheered. The curtain rose.

I gasped when I saw the stage. It was filled with wonderful equipment — a tall, shiny black box with a door in the front, a platform suspended from the ceiling, a glittering box with holes in it for a head, arms, and legs to stick out of. And a big white rabbit sitting beside a vase of blue flowers on a table covered with a red scarf.

The rabbit wasn't tied up or caged or anything. "I wonder how he keeps that rabbit from running away," Ginny whispered. "That's a trick *you* need to learn."

"You're so funny, Ginny," I said, rolling my eyes. "My sides are splitting with laughter."

"You have no sense of humor," Ginny jeered. "That's your problem."

"No. *You're* my problem," I snapped.

38

Amaz-O strode onstage. He was tall and slim, and his top hat made him seem even taller. He had long black hair and wore a black cape lined with red satin over a black tuxedo.

He tossed the cape over his shoulders and bowed.

I can't believe I'm seeing Amaz-O in person! I thought, my heart pounding with excitement. And so close — I could almost touch him!

Maybe I'll even see how some of his tricks are done, I thought. Maybe, sitting so close, I'll catch some of his secrets!

Without saying a word, Amaz-O scanned the audience. He trained his eyes on me.

My whole body shook. He's staring right at me! I gasped.

Amaz-O took a step forward and leaned toward me.

What's he doing? I thought. Is he going to talk to me?

Amaz-O leaned closer. His face was right next to mine! I cowered in my seat.

He scowled and whispered in a deep, menacing voice, "Disappear! Disappear!"

8

I shrank back.

"Disappear!" he growled again.

"Excuse me?" I gasped. I stared up at him. On TV he seemed friendly. But in person he was definitely frightening.

"Disappear!" he whispered. "I'm going to make you disappear at the end of the show. I will ask for volunteers — and I will choose you."

He didn't want me to disappear for real. He wanted me to be part of his act! I couldn't believe it!

I'll find out how he does his famous disappearing trick! I thought. Maybe I'll get to meet him after the show. Maybe he'll even tell me some of his secrets!

Ginny leaned across the table. "He's going to make you disappear forever!" she teased. "What will I tell Mom and Dad?"

I paid no attention to her. Nothing Ginny did or said could bother me now.

40

This was too cool! Just seeing Amaz-O was exciting enough. But he chose *me* to be in his show!

Maybe he could tell that I'm a magician, too, I thought.

Amaz-O began his act. "Good evening, ladies and gentlemen," he crooned. "Tonight you will see some amazing feats. You will see me do things you always thought were impossible. Are these feats real — or are they illusions? It's up to you to decide."

He waved his hands, and a wand appeared out of thin air. The audience clapped.

Then Amaz-O began to fidget with his hat, as if it felt uncomfortable on his head. "Something is wrong with my hat," he said. "It feels strange — almost as if . . ."

He lifted the hat off his head and peered into it. He showed us the inside of it. It looked perfectly normal. There was nothing inside it.

He placed it back on his head. "It's funny," he chuckled. "I thought for a minute there might be something inside my hat. I thought I felt — oh, I don't know — a flock of birds fluttering around in there."

The hat jiggled. Amaz-O appeared annoyed. "There it goes again!"

He whipped the hat off his head and stared into it. On top of his head sat a large white feather. People in the audience giggled.

"What's so funny?" Amaz-O asked. He felt the

top of his head and found the feather. "Where did that come from?" he gasped, acting amazed. Everyone laughed.

"Well, I'll try not to let this bother me," he went on, replacing his hat. "Back to the show. For my first trick — "

The hat began to shake again — slightly at first, then harder. It practically jumped off his head. The audience cracked up. Amaz-O pretended to be horrified.

He yanked the hat off his head — and out flew a whole flock of doves! They swooped over the audience and flew up to the rafters.

"I *knew* something was going on in there!" Amaz-O joked. Loud laughter and clapping.

He's the greatest, I thought, clapping along. How did he get all those birds inside his hat?

I glanced at the rabbit on stage. It sat calmly on the table, staring at Amaz-O. It almost seemed to be watching the act.

I can't wait to see his rabbit trick, I thought. Will he make the rabbit disappear? Or pull off some kind of twist?

"For my next trick I need a needle and thread," Amaz-O announced. He produced a packet of needles and a long, thick thread from one of his pockets. He picked out a needle and squinted, trying to push the thread through the eye.

"I always have trouble threading a needle," he

said. He licked the end of the thread and tried again. He couldn't get the thread to go through.

He threw up his hands in frustration. "It's impossible!" he cried. "How do tailors do it?"

The audience chuckled. I waited to see what would come next. I knew all this needle-and-thread business was a buildup to something incredible.

"So much for the *hard* way to thread a needle," Amaz-O said. "I'll show you a better way."

He snatched up the packet of needles. There must have been at least twenty needles stuck into a piece of cardboard. He popped the whole thing into his mouth. Then he dangled the long string over his mouth like a piece of spaghetti.

He slowly drew the string into his mouth, chewing. It looked as if he were eating a piece of spaghetti — with a packet of needles in his mouth, too.

"Don't you think that hurts?" Ginny whispered. "Chewing up all those needles?"

I barely nodded. I watched Amaz-O, spellbound.

Amaz-O nearly swallowed the whole string. About an inch of string stuck out between his lips. The audience waited, hushed.

He paused. Then he opened his mouth and tugged at the string. Slowly, slowly, he pulled it out of his mouth.

One by one the needles appeared — dangling from the string! Somehow he had threaded twenty needles with his tongue!

The audience gasped, then applauded. The needles flashed as Amaz-O held up the string.

"Threading needles the easy way!" he cried as he took another bow.

I've got to find out how he did that, I thought. Maybe I'll ask him after the show.

"How's the show going?" Amaz-O asked the audience. We all cheered. "I wonder how much time we have left?" He strode across the stage to the table where the rabbit and the blue flowers sat on top of the red scarf.

With a flick of his wrist, he yanked the scarf out from under the rabbit.

The rabbit didn't move. Neither did the vase of flowers. The table was now bare.

The rabbit blinked calmly. Amaz-O waved the scarf over his left hand. He let it drop — and a big red alarm clock appeared in his hand!

He glanced at the clock. "I suppose we have time for a few more tricks." He covered the clock with the scarf — and the clock disappeared.

A loud ringing suddenly erupted from the other side of the stage. I turned toward it.

The red alarm clock — floating in midair! It seemed to have flown across the stage by itself.

Amaz-O crossed the stage, grabbed the clock, and shut off the alarm.

"My clock is a little fast," he joked. "It's not time for the show to end. Not yet."

I hope not, I thought. This is the greatest magic act I've ever seen in my life!

The rest of the show was fantastic, too. Amaz-O escaped from a locked safe. He walked through a brick wall. He tapped his hat with his magic wand — and in a puff of smoke his tuxedo changed from black to yellow!

"And now for my big finale," Amaz-O announced. "I am going to make a member of the audience disappear. Are there any volunteers?"

He gazed out over the audience. No one said a word. Ginny kicked me under the table.

"Ow!" I whispered, rubbing my skin. "What did you do that for?"

"He asked for *volunteers*, you moron," she said. "That means you."

I'd been so caught up in the show, I almost forgot. I stood up. "I'd like to volunteer."

Amaz-O smiled. "Excellent, young man. Please step up on stage."

My stomach suddenly jolted with terror. I stumbled up to the stage.

Here I go, I thought nervously. Amaz-O is going to make me disappear.

I hope nothing goes wrong.

9

Amaz-O towered over me on stage. This is un-
believable, I thought. I'm on stage with the great
Amaz-O. I'm about to be part of one of his famous
tricks.

He's going to make me disappear!

I clutched my stomach, wondering, Why do I
feel so scared?

"Thanks for volunteering, young man," Amaz-O
said to me. "You must be very brave. Are your
parents here tonight?"

My parents? Uh-oh. "Um — they're here. Sure
they're here," I stammered. "But — uh — they
had to make a phone call."

Amaz-O frowned. "A phone call? In the middle
of my show?"

"Well — it was an emergency," I explained.

"Never mind. I'm glad they've stepped away.
If they knew what was about to happen to you,
they might try to stop me."

46

"Stop you?" My heart skittered nervously. But I heard the audience laughing.

Don't let him scare you, I told myself. This is just part of the act. He's joking.

I faked a laugh. "What — um — exactly — is about to happen to me?"

"I'm going to make you disappear," Amaz-O replied. "You will be transported into another dimension. I will try my best to bring you back, of course — but it doesn't *always* work."

"It doesn't?" I gulped.

He patted me on the back. "Don't worry. I've done this hundreds of times. I've only missed once or twice."

The audience chuckled. They figured he was kidding. I hoped they were right.

"Is that your sister sitting at the front table?" Amaz-O asked.

I nodded.

"Better wave good-bye to her, just in case," he warned me.

Ginny smiled and waved at me.

She can't *wait* for me to disappear! I thought bitterly. She hopes I'll never come back.

"Go on," Amaz-O urged. "Wave to her."

I smiled weakly and waved at Ginny. The audience laughed. Then Amaz-O led me to a tall black box in the center of the stage. He threw open the door. It looked like a closet inside.

"Step inside here if you would, please," he said.

I stepped inside the box. Amaz-O shut the door firmly.

It was pitch-black inside that box. I stood still, waiting for something to happen. I could hear Amaz-O talking to the audience.

"Ladies and gentlemen, this box is my own invention — the Fifth Dimension Spin-o-Rama." I heard him slap his hand against the side of the box.

"Here's how it works: my brave volunteer steps inside the box. I lock him in. I spin the box ten times — *very* fast.

"A magical force inside the box will send the boy into another dimension. He will disappear!

"I must ask for absolute silence while I do this trick. I need complete concentration."

For several seconds I heard nothing.

Then the box began to spin. "Whoa!" I cried. My body slammed against the back of the box.

It whirled around faster than any ride in an amusement park. I shut my eyes. I felt so dizzy.

I hope I don't puke, I thought. That would spoil everything.

The box kept spinning, spinning. How will the trick work? I wondered. How will I disappear?

What if he really sends me into another dimension?

But that's just talk, I told myself. Magician talk — to entertain the audience.

Isn't it?

10

The box spun faster and faster. I clutched my stomach. I saw stars dancing before my eyes.

When is it going to stop? I thought. I'm really going to be sick.

Then, suddenly, the bottom of the box dropped out from under me.

"Help!" I cried as I fell down, down, down.

"Whoa!"

I slid down a long wooden chute and landed — *thunk!* — on some kind of mattress.

I lay on my back in a daze. I heard water dripping somewhere. A dim yellow light flickered from a bare bulb on the ceiling.

I sat up, gazing around me. The room was nearly empty, dark and damp, with a cement floor. I spotted a furnace in the corner.

I'm in the basement of Midnight Mansion, I realized.

I stood up and examined the chute. So that's how the trick works, I thought. Amaz-O sets up his spinning box over a trap door in the floor of the stage. The bottom of the box drops out, and the volunteer slides down the chute and out of sight. When Amaz-O opens the door of the box — *presto!* — the volunteer has disappeared. It's so simple.

But how do I get back upstairs? I wondered. How will Amaz-O make me reappear?

Muffled applause drifted down from overhead. I could hear Amaz-O's voice, faintly. "Thank you very much, ladies and gentlemen. I must be going now. I've got to disappear into the fifth dimension and find that boy! Good night!"

The audience laughed. Then I heard music, an explosion, and loud clapping.

Amaz-O must have made himself disappear, I thought. He'll probably come sliding down this chute any minute.

I waited.

No one came sliding down the chute.

I waited a few more minutes.

Nothing.

He must have disappeared some other way, I figured.

He'll show up soon, I thought. He'll come and let me out of here. And then I'll ask him how he does that trick with the alarm clock. Maybe he'll even give me his autograph!

A few minutes later I heard chairs scraping

across the floor upstairs and a stampede of foot-steps. The show was over. The audience was leaving.

Is somebody going to let me out of here? I wondered. I was getting a little nervous. I sat down on the mattress to wait.

What's taking Amaz-O so long?

Maybe he wants to wait until everyone is gone, so no one will figure out how he did the trick. That must be it.

I waited a little longer. I heard a rustling, scuttling noise. A rat! I thought, jumping up off the mattress. I stared at the floor, watching for the rat.

The noise stopped.

Maybe it wasn't a rat, I thought, trying to calm myself. My muscles were all tense. Maybe it was only a mouse. Or a cockroach. Or my imagination.

The *drip, drip, drip* of the water somewhere in the basement was starting to drive me crazy. *Drip, drip, drip.* Like some kind of water torture.

Where is Amaz-O? When is he going to let me out of here?

I listened for signs of life upstairs. Nothing. Everything was silent up there now.

Okay, I said to myself. Everyone is gone. You can let me out now, Amaz-O.

I listened hard. I didn't hear anyone in the building.

What if Amaz-O is gone, too? I thought, panicking. What if he forgot about me and left me here?

I've got to find a way out myself, I decided.

I crept across the cement floor, keeping an eye out for rats.

It sure is dark down here, I thought.

I drifted toward the dripping sound and found myself in a room with a big laundry sink. I crossed the laundry room. On the other side I found a steep flight of steps leading to a door at the top.

Aha, I thought, feeling better now. A way out.

I climbed the rickety stairs. I reached for the doorknob and pushed.

The door didn't open. I turned the knob again and pulled.

Nothing.

The door was locked!

I rattled the door as hard as I could. I pounded on it with my fists.

"Let me out of here!" I cried. "Can anyone hear me?

"Let me out of here!"

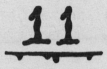

11

"Hey!" I shouted. I rattled the door. "Somebody! Get me out of here!"

How could Amaz-O do this? I thought angrily. How could he forget all about me like this?

He wouldn't lock me in the basement on purpose — would he?

No, I told myself. Why would he want to do that?

It's all just a big mistake.

I shook the door again. It loosened a little. I pushed on it, and it opened a crack.

The door was bolted from the outside with a metal hook. But the hook wasn't secure.

I'll bet I can break the door open, I realized.

I backed partway down the stairs. Then I ran to the top and threw myself against the door.

"Ow!" I grunted. The door loosened a little more. But it didn't open. And now my shoulder ached.

Then I thought the unthinkable. I couldn't be-

53

lieve I was thinking this — but I sure wished Ginny were with me.

She could've karate-kicked through that door in about five seconds. I know, because she's kicked her way into my bedroom lots of times.

Where is Ginny, anyway? I thought. She must be outside in the parking lot, waiting for me.

I had to try again. I rammed my shoulder against the door as hard as I could.

Bang! The hook broke, and the door flew open.

Excellent, I thought, rubbing my shoulder. I'm out of that horrible basement at last.

But where am I now?

A long, dark corridor.

"Hello?" I called. No answer. "Hello?"

Where is everybody? I wondered. Shouldn't there be stagehands bustling around or something?

I tiptoed down the hall. The place appeared deserted.

How could they have left me down in the basement like that? I thought angrily. How could they leave me here alone — and just go home?

At the end of the hall I saw a sliver of light. It came from under a door.

Someone's still here, I realized. Maybe it's Amaz-O!

I crept down the hall. The door had a star on it. It must be Amaz-O's dressing room! I thought. This is fantastic! I'm alone in Midnight Mansion

54

with the great Amaz-O! We'll probably stay up all night talking about magic. If I could get him to show me a few of his secrets . . .

I felt so excited and nervous my hands shook. I almost forgot about being left in the basement.

That was just a mistake, I thought. A stagehand forgot to come get me. Amaz-O must have thought I was all right. He'll probably be really glad to see me.

I stared at the star on the door. What should I do? I wondered. Should I knock? Should I call out his name?

I'll knock, I decided. I stepped to the door. *Thunk!* I tripped over something propped against the wall. A large black case with PROPERTY OF AMAZ-O written on the side.

Wow, I thought, running my fingers along the gold letters. This must be Amaz-O's magic kit! I'm touching it with my own hands!

I turned back to the door. I was about to meet my idol, my all-time hero. It was the biggest moment of my life.

I reached for the door. My hand trembled. I knocked lightly.

I waited.

Maybe he didn't hear me, I thought. I knocked again, harder this time.

Nothing.

"Hello?" I called softly, peeking into the room. Amaz-O's big white rabbit perched on the couch.

Amaz-O sat on a chair across from the rabbit. I could see his legs.

"Hello?" I called again. "It's me. From the disappearing act. Can I come in?"

I paused at the door. Amaz-O didn't answer me. Suddenly the door slammed shut in my face!

"Hey!" I cried in surprise.

A voice growled at me from the other side. "Beat it!"

"But — I'm your biggest fan! I'd just like to shake hands — "

"Beat it!" the voice snarled again. "Beat it, punk!"

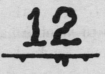

Punk? *Punk?*

Did the great Amaz-O call me a punk?

I couldn't believe it. I stood staring at the star on the door in shock.

How could Amaz-O talk to me this way? After I volunteered for his disappearing trick — and he left me locked in the basement!

What's his *problem*, anyway?

For a few seconds I couldn't move. I couldn't think. My hero had called me a punk. The greatest magician in the world — and he turned out to be a big fat jerk!

Okay, so he wasn't fat. But he was the biggest jerk I'd ever met in my whole life.

I hung my head and turned away from the door to leave. Then I saw it again — the big black case.

Amaz-O's magic kit.

Without thinking, I grabbed the case and ran.

It was heavy and awkward, but I lugged it down the hall as quickly and quietly as I could.

Why am I doing this? I wondered as I burst into the stage area.

I'm still not sure why I did it. I'd gone through so much trouble to get to the show — sneaking out of the house to meet Amaz-O. And then he was so mean to me. Maybe I wanted to get back at him.

It doesn't matter why I did it. I did it. I stole Amaz-O's magic tricks.

In the back of my mind, I knew I was headed for trouble.

I paused near the stage. Was Amaz-O following me? I listened.

Not a sound. No one coming. I swallowed hard and started running again.

I passed under the chandelier in the lobby and burst through the front door. I hope Amaz-O was the last person in the club, I thought. I hope there aren't any guards lurking around.

I didn't have time to check. I dragged the case across the gravel parking lot toward my bike.

Almost there, I told myself, panting. The parking lot was empty now. The floodlights that lit up the mansion were off. The old house lay hidden in darkness.

It must be really late, I thought. I'd better hurry home.

My bike stood where I'd left it, leaning against a rail.

I was reaching for the handlebars when a voice called "Stop!"

I froze.

I knew I was caught.

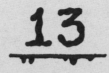

13

I heard heavy footsteps crunch toward me across the gravel parking lot.

Here they come, I thought. They've caught me red-handed with Amaz-O's bag. They'll probably arrest me.

"Where were you?" the voice called.

Ginny! I'd completely forgotten about her. Oops.

"Why are you leaving without me?" she demanded.

"Wh-why?" I stammered. What could I say? I didn't want to admit I'd forgotten all about her. "I-I wasn't leaving without you. I was looking for you. Where have *you* been?"

"Looking for *you*, Tim," she snapped. "What happened to you? You disappeared — and you never came back!"

"It's a long story," I said.

She leaned forward to read the lettering on

Amaz-O's black case. " 'Property of Amaz-O.' Where did you get that?"

"He gave it to me," I lied. "Wasn't that nice of him?"

She reached out to open the clasp that held the case shut. "Cool. What's inside?"

I stopped her hand. "I'll show it to you when we get home. It's filled with tricks. Amaz-O said I could keep it. He was grateful to me for being such a good sport in the disappearing act."

Ginny looked puzzled. "If Amaz-O gave you that case," she began, "why are those guards running this way?"

I glanced toward the mansion. Two guards charged across the parking lot, waving flashlights. Uh-oh.

I grabbed the case. "Let's get out of here!" I cried. "Quick — get on your bike. Let's ride!"

"I can't!" Ginny cried.

"Huh? Why not?"

"My bike is gone!"

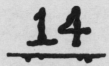

14

I jumped on my bike. "Too bad!" I cried. "See you at home!"

"Tim!" Ginny wailed. "You can't leave me here!"

I would have left her there if I could. She can take care of herself. But I knew Mom and Dad would kill me.

Besides, when the guards caught her, she'd tell on me. I'd still get in trouble.

I sat on my bike, watching the guards run right for us. Then I spotted her bike on the edge of the parking lot. "It's over there!" I told her. "Hurry!"

She raced to her bike. I balanced the case on top of my handlebars. It wasn't easy.

"Stop!" a guard yelled. Ginny and I sped out of the parking lot and down the dark street.

"Hey — stop!" the guards shouted. The beams of their flashlights blinded me for a second. I pedaled as hard as I could. Ginny darted ahead of me.

I clutched the black case with one hand and

steered with the other. The case slowed me down. The guards were gaining on us. At the first corner I zoomed left. Ginny followed.

I glanced back. The guards had stopped running. One of them bent over, panting.

"They'll never catch us now!" Ginny shouted. We biked home as fast as we could. The streets were empty and really dark. The lights were out in most of the houses.

It's after midnight, I realized. Please let Mom and Dad be asleep. If they catch us, they'll ground us till we're thirty-five! I'd almost rather be arrested.

But then, if I got arrested, Mom and Dad would *still* ground me.

We braked at our street and walked our bikes into the driveway.

"Sshhh," Ginny whispered.

"Sshhh yourself," I whispered back.

We parked the bikes in the garage. It was hard to see without the lights on. On the way into the house, Ginny tripped over the lawn mower.

"Ow!" she yelped.

"Quiet!" I snapped.

We both froze. Did Mom and Dad hear us?

Silence. "I think it's okay," I whispered.

"That hurt," Ginny whined.

"Ssshhhh!"

We sneaked into the house. "I'll hide the case in my room," I whispered.

"I want to look at it now," Ginny protested.

I shook my head. "It's mine."

"No, it's not. You have to share it with me."

"Amaz-O gave it to *me*," I insisted, even though it wasn't exactly true.

"I'm going to tell Mom and Dad," Ginny threatened. "I'll tell them you woke me up and forced me to go with you to Midnight Mansion."

"You little brat!" I cried angrily. Stupid Ginny. "Okay, I'll share it with you."

"Promise?"

"If you promise not to tell Mom and Dad."

"I promise. But you can't keep the case in your room. It's both of ours now."

I sighed. "All right. I'll hide it in the attic. Okay?"

She nodded.

"But we won't touch it until Saturday," I said. "On Saturday, we'll have plenty of time to try everything out and do it right. Deal?"

"Deal. On Saturday we'll *both* open the case, at the same time, *together*."

"Right. Now go to bed. I'll sneak it up to the attic."

We tried to be careful going up the creaky stairs. It took us about ten minutes. At the top I paused to listen for sounds from Mom and Dad's room.

"Everything is okay," Ginny whispered. "Dad is snoring."

64

She crept into her room and shut the door. I tiptoed up to the attic, lugging the black case.

I shut the attic door and switched on the light. Where can I hide this? I wondered, gazing around at all the junk. I stepped over piles of old magazines. In one corner sat my old toy chest.

Perfect, I thought, opening the chest. I pulled out a toy school bus and a couple of trucks to make room for the case.

What's in here, anyway? I wondered as I hefted Amaz-O's case. I held Amaz-O's magic kit in my hands. How could I go to sleep without seeing what's in it? How could I wait two whole days until Saturday?

Maybe I'll take a little peek inside, I thought. Just a quick one. Then I'll go to bed.

I set the case on the floor. My hands trembled as I fumbled with the clasp.

Here goes, I thought, tugging open the clasp. I pulled the case open —

And it blew up in my face!

I fell over backwards. I lay sprawled on the floor,
covering my eyes.

What happened?

Am I dead?

I opened my eyes. I squeezed my arms. I
grabbed my chest.

I'm okay, I realized.

I sat up. The case sat on the floor. No signs of
an explosion.

Carefully I crawled over to the case. I could
have sworn it had blown up. But I didn't see anything that would blow up.

Then, taped to the inside of the top flap, I saw
a little metal disk. I tapped it. It made a muffled
roar.

I examined the metal disk. It was an electronic
chip. It made an explosion sound effect when I
shook it or tapped it.

Just one of Amaz-O's tricks.

What else is in here? I wondered.

I pulled out all kinds of cool stuff. A pair of trick handcuffs. A pocket watch for hypnotizing people. Three different decks of trick cards. A rope. And a long chain of silk scarves tied together.

I wonder how all this stuff works, I thought. I'll have to fool around with it on Saturday and figure it out.

I found a small black sack that held three oval shells and a little red ball. The shell game, I realized. One of my favorite tricks. You hide the ball under one of the shells and shift them around. The audience has to guess which shell the ball is under.

They always guess wrong, because the ball isn't under *any* of the shells. The magician secretly palms the ball while he's shifting the shells around.

Gets 'em every time.

I reached into the case again. My hand brushed against something silky. I pulled it out. It was a black tuxedo jacket.

"Wow!" I gasped. "Amaz-O's own jacket!"

I had to try it on. I pulled it over my shoulders. It was too big. The shoulders drooped halfway down my arms, and the sleeves covered my hands.

But it felt great. I ran my hands over the satin lapels.

I stood up and walked around in it. A real magician's jacket. I wonder what he's got in the pockets?

I stuck my hands in the pockets. But suddenly I felt something wiggle. Along the back of the jacket, near my neck.

I shook my shoulders. The wiggling stopped.

But then I felt it again. Something came sliding down the sleeve!

I shook my arm. What is it? I thought. Is it alive?

The thing crawled along my arm. "Yuck!" I sputtered. "Get off me!" I squirmed inside the coat, trying to shake the thing off.

I had to get the jacket off — right away! I struggled to get my arms out of the sleeves.

Then something poked its head out. Out of the sleeve, near my hand.

A snake.

A live snake.

16

I clamped my mouth shut to keep from screaming. The snake felt warm and creepy against my arm. I shook my arm hard. The snake clung to me!

I gritted my teeth and shook my arm again. And again. I brushed at my sleeve with my free hand.

It wasn't working!

I shook my arm once more, as hard as I could. The snake uncoiled and slithered out of the sleeve. It dropped to the floor.

It hissed and curved around the toy chest. I watched it with a shiver.

Then I felt it again — that slippery, wriggling feeling. Something hissed near my ear and squirmed across my shoulder.

"Ohhh!" I moaned. Another snake! I slapped at it. "Get off me!"

As I tried to brush the snake away, another one slithered down my sleeve. Something slimy wriggled across my stomach and down my back. A snake popped out of an inner pocket and plopped to the floor. It started to coil around my leg.

The jacket is crammed with snakes! I realized with horror.

I thrashed my arms, frantically trying to tear off the jacket. A snake slid down the front of my shirt.

I thrashed harder, shaking my arms and legs. Now I was covered with snakes! My whole body!

I wanted to scream — but I couldn't wake Mom and Dad. A snake curled up my neck and around my head. I squirmed, desperately trying to get out of the jacket.

"Help!" I moaned. "Ohhhh — help!"

17

Snakes everywhere!

One slithered over my head. With a trembling hand, I grabbed at it and heaved it away.

Gasping in terror, I struggled out of the jacket. I tossed it on the floor. Snakes wriggled over it. Snakes wriggled over my feet. I hopped up and down. Then I hopped onto a chair. A snake coiled up the leg of the chair. It crept closer. "Go away!" I whispered. "Leave me alone!"

The snake hissed. I jumped off the chair.

Squish! My stomach turned. Did I step on a snake? I was afraid to look.

I lifted my foot and glanced down. I hadn't stepped on a snake. It was one of Ginny's old dolls.

A snake slid over the doll's face and around its neck. Another snake slithered over my shoe.

There's no escape! I realized. I've got no choice — I have to wake up Mom and Dad. What else can I do?

I hopped around the squirming, hissing snakes.

I'll get into trouble, I thought. But at least I'll be out of this snake pit!

A snake darted toward me — then suddenly froze. The room fell silent. No more hissing.

All around me the snakes stopped moving. They lay stiff on the floor. Their cold eyes stared.

What happened? Were they dead?

I glanced around, afraid to move. The floor was littered with dead snakes.

How could they all die at once? I wondered. It's so weird!

I stood there, not moving a muscle. My eyes darted around the room.

I slowly reached out my leg and tapped one of the snakes with my foot. It jiggled a little.

I took a deep breath. Should I touch it?

I got up the courage to bend close to the snake. I stuck out a finger and poked at it. Nothing happened. My heart pounded. I picked up the snake.

It lay limp in my hand. It didn't seem real.

I twisted the body. It was rubber! I examined the eyes. They were made of glass.

They're mechanical snakes, I realized.

I turned the snake over. I found a tiny wind-up key hidden under a rubber flap.

Amaz-O's jacket was rigged with wind-up snakes.

I began to breathe again. Everything is okay, I told myself. I don't have to wake up Mom and

Dad. I'm not going to get into trouble. I'm not going to be eaten alive by snakes.

When will I learn? I scolded myself. *All* of these things are just tricks. None of them is real. Amaz-O is a magician.

I gathered up the snakes and stuffed them back inside the jacket. Then I jammed the jacket into Amaz-O's magic kit. I took one last look inside the bag.

This is amazing, I thought. I've got some of Amaz-O's best tricks — right here in my own house!

I forced myself to close the kit. I'd better stop fooling around with this stuff, I thought — before anything else happens!

I'll check it all out on Saturday. In daylight, when I have plenty of time to see how it all works.

Then I'll give the kit back to Amaz-O. On Monday.

I knew I had to return the kit. It had been wrong to take it. And crazy.

If only Amaz-O hadn't been so mean to me! He used me in his act — and then he locked me in the basement! He told me to get lost. He called me a punk!

I started to get angry all over again. Amaz-O doesn't deserve to get his magic kit back, I thought.

But deep down I knew I had to return it. I

wanted to do the right thing. I'd check out the tricks, then give them back.

Of course, I didn't know then how dangerous the kit was. I didn't know the trouble it would cause.

If I had known, I would have returned the case *that night*!

18

"Another day of work," Mom sighed at the breakfast table the next morning. "I'm absolutely dreading it. Those students just drive me crazy."

Dad grabbed a doughnut and gazed out the window. "It's raining," he said unhappily. "I probably won't sell a single car today."

Ginny and I exchanged glances. Mom and Dad had no idea we had sneaked out the night before.

I slumped into a chair and ate my cereal. I was sleepy. I'm not used to staying up so late.

"You look tired, Tim," Mom said, sitting across from me. She glanced at Ginny. "So do you, honey."

"Didn't you two get any sleep?" Dad asked.

"Sure we did," I replied.

Ginny grinned. "Not that much sleep. Tim and I have a secret!"

The little brat! I kicked her under the table.

"Ow!" she cried. "Tim kicked me!"

"Don't kick your sister," Dad scolded. "I have to leave." He picked up his briefcase and kissed Mom good-bye. "Off to another day of torture. See you tonight, kids."

Dad left. Mom started clearing away the breakfast dishes. "Did you say something about a secret?" she asked.

"No!" I insisted. "Ginny didn't say anything about a secret. She said, 'Tim and I want a wee pet.'"

Mom shot me a weird look. "A what? A wee pet?"

"Yeah," I said. "You know, a little pet. A nice little kitten or something. Ginny's learning about Scotland in school now. She's picked up some Scottish words, right, Ginny? She's been running around calling everything 'wee.'"

"I have not," Ginny protested. "I've never called anything 'wee' in my life! And I'm not learning about Scotland in school!"

"Yes, you *are*," I insisted.

"What in the world are you two talking about?" Mom carried the pile of cereal bowls to the sink.

"We did a bad thing, Mom," Ginny blurted out. "Ow!" I kicked her again, but that didn't stop her.

"We sneaked out last night, Mom. We rode our bikes to Midnight Mansion to see the magic show.

We didn't get back until after midnight. I'm sorry, Mom. Please don't get angry. Tim made me do it. I didn't want to."

I covered my face with my hands. Why does Ginny have to be such a big mouth?

I'm doomed, I thought. *Doomed!*

19

"What did you say, Ginny?" Mom asked, wiping her hands on a towel. "I was running water in the sink, and I couldn't hear you."

I let out a long breath. I couldn't believe my luck. I glared at Ginny and kicked her again — really hard this time.

"Nothing, Mom," Ginny murmured. "I didn't say anything."

"You two better get ready for school," Mom said.

I pushed my chair away from the table and dragged Ginny out of hers. "We'll be ready in a minute, Mom," I said.

"What is your problem?" I whispered to Ginny in the hall. "You could've gotten us in big trouble!"

"*You* would get in trouble. Not me," Ginny replied. "You're the big brother. You *made* me go."

"I didn't make you do anything. And anyway, you promised not to tell!"

"You promised not to peek into Amaz-O's kit

until Saturday," Ginny reminded me. "But I sneaked up to the attic this morning — and I know you looked! You opened that bag! You even played with some of the stuff!"

"Me? I did not!" I lied.

"Yes, you did. One of the sleeves of a jacket was sticking out of the kit. And I found a scarf on the floor. You big fat liar!"

"So what? You'll still get to see the stuff on Saturday."

"You promised," Ginny repeated. She flicked my nose. "Boi-oi-oing."

I stormed into my room. There's no arguing with Ginny. She does whatever she wants — promise or no promise.

She's always getting me into trouble, I thought angrily. She drives me crazy! I wish there were some way I could pay her back. Some way to pay her back for everything.

Little did I realize I would soon find it.

20

"Are you sure you kids don't want to go to the antiques show with us?" Dad asked. "You might see some neat old junk there."

"We're sure," I insisted. Saturday morning had arrived, and all I could think about was Amaz-O's magic kit. I couldn't wait to get my hands on it.

I wished my parents would hurry up and leave.

"All right," Mom said, kissing Ginny and then me. "There's tuna salad in the fridge for lunch. We won't be back until dinnertime."

"Be good," Dad added.

"*I'll* be good," Ginny declared. "I don't know about *Tim*."

I tried to shove her, but she dodged me. "I'll be good," I promised. "I'm always good."

Mom rolled her eyes. "Just don't fight too much," she said. " 'Bye."

Ah. At last. As soon as they were gone, I raced to the phone and dialed Foz's number.

"The coast is clear," I told him. "Come on over."

I'd told Foz all about the show at Midnight Mansion and Amaz-O's magic kit. He begged me to let him see the cool tricks in Amaz-O's bag.

As soon as Foz arrived, we all trooped up to the attic. Ginny made a beeline for the magic kit. I blocked her.

"Heee-ya!" She leaped into a pre-karate chop stance. "Out of my way!"

"Ginny — wait!" I pleaded. "There's a lot of weird stuff in that bag. Let me show it to you my way."

"Okay." She relaxed. "But don't forget you're supposed to share it with me."

I pulled up two chairs. "You guys sit here," I said to Ginny and Foz. "And get ready for the greatest magic show in the history of the world!"

I reached into the toy chest and pulled out Amaz-O's magic kit. I held it up in front of Foz and Ginny. "First," I began in my magician voice, "gaze deeply into the magic trove."

I held the bag near their faces. They stared at it. I yanked it open.

Kaboom! It made the exploding sound, just as it did the first time I opened it.

Ginny and Foz fell off their chairs!

"What happened?" Foz moaned, clutching his head. "That thing blew up in my face!"

I cracked up. "It's only a sound effect," I explained.

"Not funny," Ginny complained.

"You should have seen your faces," I said gleefully. I reached into the black sack that held the three shells and the red ball. I set the shells in a row on a small table.

"Watch closely," I said. I held up the red ball. "See this ball? I'll place it under one of these shells." I pretended to tuck the ball under the middle shell. But secretly I palmed the ball and flicked it up my sleeve.

I began moving the shells over the table, shifting their places.

"Keep your eyes on the middle shell," I instructed. Then I stopped moving the shells.

"Which shell is the ball under?" I asked.

"That one," Ginny said, pointing to the shell on the right.

"Are you *sure*?" I prompted. "Foz, where do you think the ball is?"

"The same one as Ginny," he said. "I watched it the whole time."

"If you say so," I said. I was sure the ball wasn't under that shell — it wasn't under any of them. I felt the ball rubbing against my wrist.

I lifted the shell — and gasped. There *was* a ball under there. A red ball, just like the one I'd palmed.

"I was right!" Ginny crowed. "That's a stupid trick."

"But this is impossible!" I cried. I let the first ball fall out of my sleeve. I *had* palmed it.

"This is very strange," I muttered. "Let me try again."

I dropped the first ball on the floor. I picked up the second ball and pretended to slip it under a different shell. I palmed the ball and tucked it up my sleeve again.

"Here we go," I said, shifting the shells all over the table. I slid the shells around a little longer, then stopped.

"The ball is under the first shell," Foz said.

"Yes, the first shell," Ginny agreed.

"This time you're wrong!" I cried. I lifted the first shell. Another red ball!

Ginny sneered. "You're a real ace, Tim."

"Wait a second," I said. I lifted up the other two shells. All three of them had red balls under them!

"This isn't working at all," I grumbled. I set the shells down, then lifted them again. More balls! There were now three balls under each shell!

"This isn't the shell game I know." I was mystified. "This must be some other trick."

"It's way better than your dumb trick," Ginny said. "Those balls are coming out of nowhere!"

The shells began to dance as balls bubbled out of them like popcorn. Ten balls. Twenty balls.

Little red balls covered the table and bounced to the floor.

"They're still coming!" Foz cried in amazement. "We're going to be up to our necks in red balls!"

"How do I stop this thing?" I wondered.

Can I stop it?

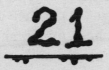

21

I snatched up the shells and tossed them into their black sack. Then I grabbed all the red balls I could and stuffed them in, too.

"Help me, you guys!" I pleaded.

Ginny and Foz fell to their knees, gathering up red balls. We shoved them all into the sack. I pulled the string that closed it and dropped it into the magic kit.

The black sack kept bubbling. Red balls started bursting out of it.

"Stop that!" I yelled. I reached into the magic case and pulled out the first thing I touched. Then I snapped the case shut.

"I don't really get that trick," Ginny complained.

"Here's another trick," I said. "This one will be better." In my hand I held a flattened top hat. "Let's see what this does."

I punched the top hat open and placed it on my head.

"It's just a hat," Foz said, fidgeting. "It's kind of hot up here. Can we go down to the kitchen and get something to eat?"

"You guys don't get it," I said. "This is *Amaz-O's* magic case! Okay, so I don't know how anything works yet. Once we figure it out, we could put on the best magic show ever! I could become a famous magician!"

"And I could be a famous magician's sister." Ginny yawned. "Big deal."

"That hat looks way cool on you," Foz said. "Now can we get something to eat?"

"I'm hungry, too," Ginny added.

"Wait!" I cried. I felt something move under the hat. I whipped it off.

"A white dove!" Foz cried.

"That's a good trick," Ginny admitted.

I shook the dove off my head. "How do you get it back in the hat?" I asked. Before I had a chance to try, another dove popped out of the hat.

I set the second dove on the floor. "There's another one!" Foz shouted.

A third dove flew out of the hat and settled on top of an old lamp. Out popped a fourth, and a fifth . . .

Foz started laughing. "These tricks are totally out of control!"

"This is no joke, Foz!" I snapped.

"We're going to be in major trouble," Ginny

warned. "We've got to find a way to get rid of these birds!"

The attic was quickly filling up with flapping, fluttering doves — and they kept coming. I knew we had to get rid of them — but how?

"Maybe there's something in here that will help." I ripped open the magic case. *Kaboom!* It made that stupid exploding sound again. Dozens of little red balls flew into my face.

"I'm really getting sick of this," I muttered.

I brushed away piles of balls. I pulled out a long black stick with a white tip. A magic wand!

"Maybe this will help!" I cried. I hoped it would. The attic was a total mess — white doves and red balls everywhere.

"This is the answer," I declared. "Amaz-O probably uses this wand to make the magic stop."

"I hope you're right," Ginny said. "If that doesn't work, you and I are going to have to run away from home."

"It'll work," I insisted. "It's got to."

I waved the wand in the air. "Stop!" I shouted. "Everything stop!"

22

Did it work?

No.

More doves flew out of the hat. More red balls bubbled out of the black sack.

"That magic wand is the only thing in there that *doesn't* work!" Foz joked.

"Be quiet!" I snapped. "I've got to think!"

"Yikes!" Ginny screamed. "A snake!"

She pointed at the magic case. A snake slithered out of it. Then a second, a third.

The mechanical snakes had come back to life!

Hissing snakes soon covered the floor, wriggling over the bouncing red balls. Dove feathers fell from the ceiling. The attic was so crowded I could hardly see across the room.

Ginny yelped as a snake began to crawl up her leg. "Let's get out of here!" she cried.

She yanked open the attic door. She and Foz hurried downstairs. I grabbed the magic case and followed them. A snake slithered after me.

"Get back in there!" I yelled. I picked up the snake and threw it into the attic room. I shut the door. I pushed on it to make sure it was closed. Then I ran downstairs and out to the backyard.

A gust of March wind slapped my face. Ginny's long hair flew out behind her.

"Snakes — ick!" she squealed. "Tim — what are we going to do? When Mom and Dad see the attic, we're dead meat!"

Foz stared at the magic case. "What did you bring that out for? It's dangerous!"

"It's okay if we stay outside," I told him. "So what if a bunch of birds comes out? They'll fly away."

I wasn't as sure about that as I sounded. But I couldn't give Amaz-O's case back without seeing everything in it first. I just couldn't.

"Hurry up, Tim," Ginny whined. "I'm starving. It's lunchtime!"

"Wait. Wait." I opened the magic case. *Kaboom!* It didn't sound so loud outside — especially with the wind blowing as hard as it was.

I held the magic wand poised between my fingers. What does this thing do? I wondered.

I waved it around, trying out new magician names. "The Great Incredible-O. Mister Terrifico — that's not bad. Get out of there, Ginny!" She was rummaging through the magic kit.

"You promised we'd share it, remember?" she snapped. Then her face brightened. "Hey! Great!"

She pulled a carrot out of Amaz-O's bag. "Just what I needed — something to eat."

"Put that back!" I ordered.

"It's still fresh," she said. "Yum!"

She opened her mouth, ready to bite the carrot.

"Ginny — no!" I cried. "Maybe you shouldn't eat that. Maybe — "

Ginny never listens to me.

She crunched down on the carrot.

A flash of white light blinded me for a moment.

When my eyes focused, I saw the most amazing thing I'd ever seen in my life!

23

The carrot dropped to the grass. Ginny's nose twitched. Then she began to shrink.

As she shrank, her hair turned from blond to white. Her nose turned pink. White fur and whiskers sprouted from her face. She grew smaller, furrier, whiter. . . .

"I don't believe it!" Foz gasped. "Your sister — she's a rabbit!"

Ginny sat on the grass, twitching her little pink nose. She stared at me with her rabbity eyes. She waved her little paws and made angry, rabbity noises.

"Man, she is *steamed!*" Foz cried.

I was stunned. "I wished it," I murmured. "And now it's come true."

"What are you talking about?" Foz demanded. He grabbed me by the shoulders. "Get it together, Tim. We've got to do something! What's going to happen when your parents get home?"

"I told Ginny I'd turn her into a rabbit," I explained, still dazed. "To get back at her for ruining all my magic shows. And now she *is* a rabbit!"

Ginny the rabbit rose on her hind legs, gesturing angrily at me. Then she bounced up and thumped my shin with one of her big rabbit feet.

"Ow!" I cried. "That hurts as much as one of her karate kicks!"

"Look in the kit, Tim," Foz urged me. "There's got to be some way to change her back."

"You're right. There's got to be!" My eyes fell on the carrot in the grass. "The carrot," I said. "When Ginny bit it, she turned into a rabbit. But maybe if a rabbit bites it, it turns into a girl!"

Foz shook his head. "Huh?"

I snatched up the carrot. "We've got to try it. There's nothing to lose, right? She's already a rabbit. What else could happen to her?"

I shoved the end of the carrot toward Ginny's mouth. "Come on, Ginny. Take another bite."

She stared at the carrot suspiciously. She clamped her mouth shut and turned her face away.

"You little brat!" I shouted. "You *want* me to get in trouble, don't you! You want to stay a rabbit just to get me in trouble!"

Foz grabbed the carrot out of my hand. "Calm down, Tim. You're scaring her!"

Ginny's long rabbit ears perked up — she heard something. I heard it, too. A car coming. Pulling into the driveway!

"Hurry, Ginny!" I cried. "I think Mom and Dad

are home. Take a bite of the carrot. It'll turn you back into a girl. I know it will!"

Ginny eyed me suspiciously. She sniffed the carrot with her twitchy pink nose.

"Hurry!" I shouted again.

She opened her mouth and took a nibble of carrot.

Foz and I watched her in a panic. "Please let it work," I prayed. "Please let it work!"

24

Ginny's rabbit nose twitched. Her ears stood straight up. Then they flopped down.

Nothing happened. She was still a rabbit.

"Mom and Dad!" I cried. "They're here! Foz — stay with Ginny. If Mom and Dad ask, say she's your sister's rabbit!"

I ran to the driveway. A car was backing out — not Mom and Dad. Just somebody turning around in our driveway.

Whew. Close one.

The wind gusted as I ran back to Foz and Ginny. Foz was on his knees, digging through the magic kit. Ginny hopped up and down impatiently.

The magic wand lay in the grass. Maybe this will work now, I hoped, picking it up. I've got to change her back!

I waved the wand over Ginny. "Turn my sister back into a girl!" I cried.

Nothing.

"Maybe you need to say the spell in a rhyme," Foz suggested. "Magicians always do that."

"Okay." I waved the wand again. "Let me think. . . . Magic wand, winds that whirl, turn Ginny back into a girl!"

The wand began to shake. "Something's happening!" I shouted.

The white tip of the wand broke open. Out popped a white silk handkerchief.

"Wow!" Foz gasped. A blue one flew out, then a red one, then a yellow one. The wind blew them away before I could catch them.

I turned back to Ginny. Still a rabbit.

"It didn't work," I said unhappily. I tossed the wand into the grass. "It only makes stupid handkerchiefs."

I crossed over to the magic case. Ginny leaped at me, trying to bite my leg.

"Watch out!" I warned her. "I'm trying to help you!"

She twitched her nose in disgust.

Foz moved aside as I dove into the magic kit. I dumped everything out. A slip of paper tumbled out of a pocket in the case.

I snatched it up. At the top of the paper I saw the word INSTRUCTIONS.

"Look!" I cried. "Instructions!" I patted Ginny between the ears. "I'll have you back to normal in a second."

I raised the paper to read what it said. " 'Instructions. To use the magic top hat . . .' No. That's not what I need right now. . . ."

"Hurry, Tim!" Foz said.

I scanned the paper, searching for anything about rabbits. "Here's something!" I announced. " 'The magic carrot . . .' "

Just then a strong gust of wind blasted across the yard. The paper flew out of my hands.

"No!" I shouted, grasping for the paper. "I need that!" I watched helplessly as it flew out of my reach — high up into the sky.

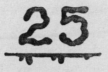

25

"Get that paper!" I screamed. The wind blew it across the yard. I darted after it.

Foz zoomed ahead of me, yelling, "I've got it! I've got it!" The paper floated within his reach. He dove for it.

Whoosh! Another strong gust of wind. The paper fluttered away. Foz fell flat on his face.

I ran past him, following the paper. It blew across my neighbor's yard.

"Get it!" Foz shouted, racing after me. "It's headed for the woods!"

The wind died for a minute. The paper settled on the grass.

I pounced on it. But the wind picked up before I landed. The paper blew away again.

"Rats!" I cried.

"There it goes!" Foz shouted. The paper drifted toward the stream.

The paper floated above the stream, then

landed in the water. Foz zipped across the yard to grab it.

"Don't let it get wet!" I screamed.

Too late. The paper was soaked.

"I've got it!" Foz shouted. He leaned over the stream and snatched at the paper. But the current carried it away.

Foz and I chased it down the stream, panting. But we couldn't run as fast as the current.

"It's getting away," I huffed. A few seconds later we lost sight of it.

Foz and I collapsed on the ground.

"That's it," I groaned. "We'll never get it back now. So how do I turn Ginny back into a girl?"

Foz heaved himself to his feet and pulled me up by the hand. "Don't panic, Tim. Panicking isn't going to help."

Great advice.

We hurried back to Ginny. I hoped maybe she'd magically turned back into a girl while we were gone. No such luck.

Ginny knew we hadn't found the instructions. She bounced around the yard, squealing angry rabbit squeals.

Foz rubbed his short hair as he watched her. "Boy, she's really stressed," he said.

I fell to my knees to talk to her. "Don't worry, Ginny," I soothed. "I've got an idea. I'm going to take you to Amaz-O right now. He'll turn you back into a girl. I'm sure he will."

With one of her long rabbit ears, Ginny flicked my nose. She couldn't say "Boi-oi-oing." She didn't have to. I knew what she meant.

"Let's pick this stuff up," I said to Foz. We began to gather all the tricks off the grass and pile them into Amaz-O's magic case. "Amaz-O won't want to help us if I don't give him back his magic kit."

Foz took my bike, balancing the magic kit on the handlebars. I picked up Ginny. "Come on, little rabbit sister," I cooed. She let me pull her up by the back — then nipped me on the wrist!

"Ow!" I dropped her. "Do you want me to help you or not?"

She hopped up and down angrily. I knew what she was thinking. If I didn't change her back into a girl, I'd be in as much trouble as she was. I had no choice.

I reached for her again. "Don't bite me this time," I warned her. "Or I'll put a muzzle over that little snout of yours."

She squirmed in my arms but didn't bite. I set her in the basket on her bike.

"To Midnight Mansion," I told Foz. We set off, pedaling hard against the strong wind.

I rode through town in a daze. Ginny's long white ears waved in my face.

Amaz-O's words rang in my ears. "Beat it, punk!" he'd said. I wondered if he'd really help me.

He's got to, I told myself. He'll be glad to get his magic kit back.

I'll make him help, I decided. I won't give him the kit until he turns Ginny back into a girl.

We pulled into the parking lot in front of Midnight Mansion. The old castle looked just as scary in the daytime as it did at night. There were no floodlights casting shadows on the stone towers. But the gray, vine-covered walls gave the place a spooky, abandoned feeling.

I skidded to a stop in front of the mansion. Foz carried the magic kit. I grabbed Ginny out of the bike basket.

"Behave," I warned her as we climbed the front steps to the mansion. "Remember, I'm trying to help you. Don't go biting me or anything."

She twitched her nose at me. She lifted her little rabbit lips and bared her tiny rabbit teeth.

"Go ahead — bite me," I whispered. "See how you like spending the rest of your life as a rabbit. You don't even *like* lettuce!"

She closed her mouth and twitched her nose again. It doesn't matter whether she's a girl or a rabbit, I thought. Either way she's a pain in the neck.

We stopped at the top of the steps.

"Oh, no!" I gasped. "I don't believe it!"

The sign on the front door read SORRY, WE'RE CLOSED.

26

"No!" I cried. I banged my forehead against the door.

Foz said, "This place gives me the creeps. It looks like Count Dracula's castle." He shivered. "Let's get out of here."

He set the magic case down. "Amaz-O's magic kit is so heavy. Do you think we can leave it by the door?"

I glared at him. "*No*, we can't leave it by the door. And we're not going home. Not yet."

I squeezed Ginny in my arms, thinking. "Okay, so the place is closed. But Amaz-O could be in there, rehearsing or something. Right?"

"He could be, I guess," Foz said. "But chances are — "

"We've got to take that chance," I insisted. I tried the front door. Locked. Of course.

"There must be another way in," I said. "A back

door or something." I dashed down the steps and around the side of the club.

"Bring the case, Foz!" I ordered.

He followed me, lugging the kit. I kept my eyes peeled for guards.

At the back of the mansion we found a door. I tried it. It opened easily!

We crept inside. We found ourselves in the club's kitchen. It was long, narrow, and shiny clean. The lights were off, but we could see by the light from a window at one end.

Foz paused in front of a huge, stainless steel refrigerator. "I'll bet they've got some great food in here," he whispered. "Lemon meringue pie or something."

I tugged at his arm. "This is no time for a snack!" I snapped. "Come on!"

We left the kitchen and entered a long, dark hallway. I recognized that hall. It was the same hallway I'd walked down after my escape from the basement — the *first* time Amaz-O let me down.

"There'd better not be a second time," I muttered under my breath.

We tiptoed down the dark hall. Up ahead I saw the door to Amaz-O's dressing room. It was half-open. A dim light spilled out into the hallway.

Yes! I thought to myself. That's a good sign.

With Ginny in my arms, I crept up to the door. Please, please let him be in there, I prayed. Please be here, Amaz-O. Please help us

I stopped in front of the door. I took a deep breath.

"Mr. Amaz-O? Are you here?"

27

No reply.

I tried again. "Mr. Amaz-O? Hello?"

"He's not here," Foz said. "Let's go."

"Shhh!" I pushed the door open and crept into the dressing room. One small lamp cast a dim pool of light on the dressing table. The great Amaz-O sat on the couch, his left side facing the door. He was staring at the wall. He didn't seem to notice us.

"Mr. Amaz-O?" I said politely. "It's me again. The kid you made disappear in your magic show."

I thought Amaz-O would turn his head to face us now, but he didn't. He didn't do anything. He just sat there.

Man, I thought. He really hates kids. Or he hates his fans. Or he hates all people. Or something.

When I become a great magician, I vowed, I won't be like Amaz-O. I won't let my fame go to my head. I'll be nice to people. This is ridiculous.

I didn't care what Amaz-O's problem was. I needed his help — badly. And I wouldn't give up until I got it.

I stepped farther into the dressing room. "Mr. Amaz-O, I'm sorry to bother you. But I really need your help. It's important."

Amaz-O didn't move. He stared at the wall. Silent.

"Do you think he's asleep?" Foz whispered.

I shrugged. I took another breath and crept closer to the couch.

"I know you told me to beat it," I said. "I wouldn't bother you if it wasn't a matter of life and death — I swear."

Still no response. I turned back to Foz, who cowered in the doorway. He looked as if he were ready to run for it. I waved him into the room.

Foz stepped in. He set the magic kit on the floor, shaking.

I stared at Amaz-O. He ignored me. Who does he think he is? I thought angrily. He can't treat me this way! I'm not leaving until he helps me turn Ginny back into a girl.

I steeled myself and approached the magician. He didn't look at me. I tapped him on the shoulder.

He toppled over onto his side. *Thunk!*

Foz gasped. "Is he — ? Is he — ?"

I peered at the body on the couch. "He isn't alive!" I cried. "Amaz-O isn't alive!"

"Oh, no!" Foz was wringing his hands in terror. "Oh, no! He's dead! He's dead! Help!"

"He's not dead," I said. "He's a dummy!

"Amaz-O is nothing but a big wooden puppet!"

28

How could it be possible? I stared at the puppet on the couch. I couldn't resist touching its cheek — then pinching it — just to be sure.

Oh, wow!

It was true. Amaz-O was made of wood.

Foz sputtered, "But — I saw him on TV. He looked totally real."

"And I saw him live," I said. "On stage. I stood right next to him, and he made me disappear!"

How can this be? I wondered. How can the greatest magician in the world be a puppet?

"This can't be the guy you saw," Foz insisted, poking at the dummy. "This is probably just a dummy he keeps around for fun. The real Amaz-O has got to be around here somewhere."

Rabbit Ginny squirmed angrily in my arms. "Calm down," I ordered, trying to pet her.

She growled. I've never heard of a rabbit growling before. Only a Ginny-rabbit would growl.

Amaz-O, my idol, I thought bitterly. What a

fake he turned out to be. Not only was he a jerk to me — he's not even a real person! He's a puppet!

"What are we going to do?" Foz asked.

I shook my head. I had no idea. "Now I'll never get Ginny changed back into a girl," I said. "Mom and Dad are going to *murder* me."

"Why don't you tell them she ran away?" Foz suggested. "They'll never believe you turned her into a rabbit, anyway."

"Why would she run away?" I demanded. "She was their little darling. She could do no wrong. *I'm* the one who should run away."

Foz lifted the Amaz-O puppet's head, studying it. "I wonder how this thing works. . . ." he said.

A low voice suddenly growled, "Hey, punk — I told you to beat it!"

I froze. "Did you say something, Foz?" I asked.

He shook his head, eyes wide. He'd heard the voice, too.

"So beat it! Get out of here!" the voice growled.

I glanced around the room. I didn't see anyone.

"Did the puppet talk?" I asked Foz.

"I — I don't think so," he stammered. "The voice came from the other side of the room."

"The puppet didn't talk, dummy," the voice grumbled. I turned to find it. I gazed across the room. Amaz-O's white rabbit sat on a chair in front of the dressing table.

"I told you to get lost. Now get lost!" the rabbit growled.

"Tim — did — did you see that?" Foz stammered. "I think that rabbit talked."

"Of course I talked, stupid," the rabbit snarled.

"You talked?" I echoed in amazement.

"I guess that thing on the couch isn't the only dummy in this room," the rabbit snapped. "I can do lots of things. I'm a magician."

Foz and I stared at the rabbit, stunned. Even Ginny stopped squirming in my arms.

"You're not a magician," Foz said. "You're a rabbit."

The rabbit's ears twisted. "Duh. You guys are really quick. You know that?"

"You don't have to be so mean," I protested.

"*You* don't have to be so stupid," the rabbit replied. "I may *look* like a rabbit. But so does your little sister. Am I right?"

"He's got a point," Foz admitted.

"I am the great Amaz-O," the rabbit announced. "In person. That dummy on the couch is a puppet I had built to look like me — the old me."

My jaw fell open. "*You're* Amaz-O? What happened to you?"

The rabbit sighed. "It's a long story. Let's just say I had a rival — a real powerful one. A sorcerer, actually."

Foz gasped. "A sorcerer? Do they really exist?"

109

"I'm telling you about one, aren't I?" the rabbit shouted.

"Yes, but — "

"So be quiet and listen to the story," Amaz-O, the rabbit, grumbled. "If you'd stop talking you might learn something."

Amaz-O sure was a grouch.

"Anyway, long story short," Amaz-O went on. "This sorcerer guy — Frank — "

"A sorcerer named Frank?" I cut in. I didn't mean to interrupt. It just slipped out.

The rabbit glared at me. "*Yes*, a sorcerer named Frank. You got a problem with that?"

I shook my head.

"Can I finish talking now? You got any more stupid questions?"

Foz and I both shook our heads.

"This guy's named Foz — " Amaz-O gestured toward Foz " — and you want to make fun of a guy named Frank."

"I'm sorry," I said. "I didn't mean to make fun of Frank."

"He's a very powerful guy," Amaz-O said. "I'm proof of that."

The rabbit hopped out of the chair, crossed the dressing room, and sat on the couch next to the dummy.

"Here's what happened," he began. "I was at the height of my fame. I was the most brilliant magician in the world. I made appearances on all the top TV shows. I had millions of fans. Dopey little kids like you looked up to me."

"Hey!" I protested. "Stop calling us dopey."

Amaz-O ignored me. He continued, "My tricks were the most amazing anyone had ever seen. And Frank was jealous. He was a sorcerer, working alone in a basement. He could cast amazing spells — but he was kind of ugly, with a high-pitched voice. People didn't take him seriously.

"He wanted to be famous like me, but he wasn't. So he turned me into a rabbit. Very funny, right? Ha ha. Turn the magician into a rabbit. Yuk, yuk, yuk."

Foz and I exchanged baffled glances. Amaz-O was turning out to be a little weird.

"I'm not powerful enough to reverse Frank's spell," Amaz-O went on. "I'm a magician, not a sorcerer. But I refused to let him stop me. So I built that mechanical dummy over there. I made him look just like me. And I kept on doing my shows, just as before."

"So you control the puppet?" Foz asked. "You make it look as if he's the magician, performing all the tricks?"

"I just said that, didn't I?" Amaz-O snapped. "Are you hard-of-hearing, kid?"

"You're really rude, you know that, Amaz-O?" I said. I was getting sick of his put-downs. "You're the rudest person — or rabbit, or whatever — I ever met in my life!"

Amaz-O's long ears drooped. "Hey — I'm sorry," he said. "Being a rabbit gets on my nerves. But also, I can't let people get too close — you know? I don't want anyone to find out my secret. It could ruin me."

Ginny squirmed in my arms again. I'd nearly forgotten all about her. I realized I'd better hurry up and ask Amaz-O to help me change her back.

"We're in terrible trouble, Amaz-O," I said, holding Ginny toward him. "This is my sister, Ginny. She ate some of the carrot that was in your magic kit — "

"So you confess, do you? You stole my magic kit!"

"I — I only borrowed it," I stammered. "I brought it back — see? I'm sorry."

"I'll bet you are," Amaz-O snapped.

"Can you help us, Amaz-O?" I pleaded. "Please, can you help me turn Ginny back into a girl?"

Amaz-O studied Ginny with his beady rabbit eyes. I held my breath waiting for his answer.

He settled deeper into the couch and shook his head. "Sorry," he said. "There's nothing I can do for her."

29

"Noooo!" I moaned, sinking into a chair. "You were my last chance. I'm doomed!"

"You didn't let me finish," Amaz-O said. "There's nothing I can do for her — because the magic will wear off by itself."

"Yo! All right!" Foz exclaimed happily. He shot both fists into the air.

"But when?" I asked. "My parents are coming home soon."

"How many bites of the carrot did she eat?" Amaz-O asked.

"Two," I replied.

"How long ago?"

"About an hour ago," I answered.

"Okay," Amaz-O said. "She should turn back into a girl in half an hour. Do you feel better now?"

I nodded and sighed with relief. That was a close one, I thought. But everything is going to be okay.

"Hey — " Foz said, jumping up. "We'd better hurry up and take Ginny home — before she turns back into a girl. We don't have enough bikes to go around!"

I pushed Ginny into his arms. "Take her home, Foz," I said. "I'll be there in a few minutes." I wanted to talk to Amaz-O a little longer.

Clutching Ginny in his arms, Foz hurried out of the dressing room. "Don't stay too long," he called over his shoulder. "I don't want to be alone with Ginny when she turns back into a girl. I have a feeling she's going to be in the mood to karate-chop somebody!"

In reply, Ginny beat her hind legs against his chest.

"I'm right behind you," I promised. Foz disappeared down the dark hallway.

"Listen, Amaz-O," I said. "I'm really sorry I stole your magic bag. I know it was a terrible thing to do."

"Shove this stupid dummy aside and sit down on the couch," Amaz-O said. I moved the dummy and sat down next to Amaz-O.

"You really love magic, don't you?" he said.

My heart started pounding. This was the heart-to-heart magician talk I'd been hoping to have with Amaz-O all along!

"It's my dream to be a magician," I told him. "A great magician like you. I'd do anything. Anything!"

"Well, you were great in the show the other

night," Amaz-O said. "You disappeared very well, kid."

"Thanks."

Amaz-O sat quietly for a moment. He seemed to be thinking.

"Say, kid — " he said at last. "How would you like to join the act? I'm getting really tired of working with that big wooden dummy over there."

"Me?" Now my heart was really racing. "You want me to join the act?" I got so excited I jumped off the couch. Then I quickly sat down again. "Do you mean it, Amaz-O? Do you think I could?"

Amaz-O hopped over to the dressing room door. He kicked it shut.

"Why don't we give you a try. . . ."

30

And that's how I joined Amaz-O's act. I was so excited about being a magician, I said yes without even thinking about it. I guess I should've asked a few questions first.

Don't get me wrong. I love being on stage in front of clapping, cheering audiences.

But I don't like hiding inside the black top hat. And I hate it when the Amaz-O dummy pulls me up too hard by the ears. That really hurts.

I also hate it when they forget to clean my cage. Sometimes they forget about it for days!

I guess I made a little mistake. See, when Amaz-O said he was tired of working with the big dummy, I thought he wanted me to take the dummy's place.

I didn't realize he wanted to retire — and have me take *his* place!

I'm not complaining. Amaz-O gives me plenty of juicy lettuce and all the carrots I can eat. I even have a stage name of my own now. At last. It

may not be my first choice, but it's still a professional name — "Fluffy."

The best part is, I'm on stage every night in a
real magic act! My dream — my all-time dream!

How many kids — er — I mean, rabbits — can
say their all-time dream came true at age twelve?

I'm really lucky — don't you agree?

About the Author

R.L. STINE is the author of over three dozen best-selling thrillers and mysteries for young people. Recent titles for teenagers include *I Saw You That Night!*, *Call Waiting*, *Halloween Night II*, *The Dead Girlfriend*, and *The Baby-sitter IV*, all published by Scholastic. He is also the author of the *Fear Street* series.

Bob lives in New York City with his wife, Jane, and fifteen-year-old son, Matt.

Add *more*

Goosebumps®

to your collection . . .
A chilling preview of
what's next from
R.L. STINE

EGG MONSTERS FROM MARS

Three girls from Brandy's class came running across the lawn. I recognized them. They were the girls I call the Hair Sisters. They're not sisters. But they spend all their time in Brandy's room after school doing each other's hair.

Dad moved slowly across the grass toward them. He had his camcorder up to his face. The three Hair Sisters waved to the camera and yelled, "Happy Birthday, Brandy!"

Dad tapes all our birthdays and vacations and big events. He keeps the tapes on a shelf in the den. We never watch them.

The sun beamed down. The grass smelled sweet and fresh. The spring leaves on the trees were just starting to unfurl.

"Okay — everyone follow me to the back!" Brandy ordered.

The kids lined up in twos and threes, carrying their baskets. Anne and I followed behind them. Dad walked backwards, busily taping everything.

Brandy led the way to the backyard. Mom was waiting there. "The eggs are hidden everywhere," Mom announced, sweeping her hand in the air. "Everywhere you can imagine."

"Okay, everyone!" Brandy cried. "At the count of three, the egg hunt begins! *One* — "

Anne leaned down and whispered in my ear. "Bet you five dollars I collect more eggs than you."

I smiled. Anne always knows how to make things more interesting.

"*Two* — "

"You've got a bet!" I told her.

"*Three!*" Brandy called.

The kids all cheered. The hunt for hidden eggs was on.

They all began hurrying through the backyard, bending down to pick up eggs. Some of them moved on hands and knees through the grass. Some worked in groups. Some searched through the yard on their own.

I turned and saw Anne stooping down, moving quickly along the side of the garage. She already had three eggs in her basket.

I can't let her win! I told myself. I sprang into action.

I ran past a cluster of girls around the old doghouse. And I kept moving.

I wanted to find an area of my own. A place where I could grab up a bunch of eggs without having to compete with the others.

I jogged across the tall grass, making my way to the back. I was all alone, nearly to the creek when I started my search.

I spotted an egg hidden behind a small rock. I had to move fast. I wanted to win the bet.

I bent down, picked it up, and quickly dropped it in my basket.

Then I knelt down, set my basket on the ground, and started to search for more eggs.

But I jumped up when I heard a scream.

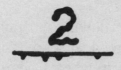

2

"Aaaaaiiiiii!"

The scream rang through the air.

I turned back toward the house. One of the Hair Sisters was waving her hand wildly, calling to the other girls. I grabbed up my basket and ran toward her.

"They're not hard-boiled!" I heard her cry as I came closer. And I saw the drippy yellow yolk running down the front of her white T-shirt.

"Mom didn't have time to hard-boil them," Brandy announced. "Or to paint them. I know it's weird. But there just wasn't time."

I raised my eyes to the house. Mom and Dad had both disappeared inside.

"Be careful," Brandy warned her party guests. "If you crack them — "

She didn't finish her sentence. I heard a wet *splat.*

Then laughter.

A boy had tossed an egg against the side of the doghouse.

"Cool!" one of the girls exclaimed.

Anne's big sheepdog, Stubby, came running out of the doghouse. I don't know why he likes to sleep in there. He's almost as big as the house.

But I didn't have time to think about Stubby.

Splat.

Another egg exploded, this time against the garage wall.

More laughter. Brandy's friends thought it was really hilarious.

"Egg fight! Egg fight!" two boys started to chant.

I ducked as an egg went sailing over my head. It landed with a *craaack* on the driveway.

Eggs were flying everywhere now. I stood there and gaped in amazement.

I heard a shrill shriek. I spun around to see that two of the Hair Sisters had runny yellow egg oozing in their hair. They were shouting and tugging at their hair and trying to pull the yellow gunk off with both hands.

Splat! Another egg hit the garage.

Craaack! Eggs bounced over the driveway.

I ducked down and searched for Anne. She probably went home, I figured. Anne enjoys a good laugh. But she's twelve, much too sophisticated for a babyish egg fight.

Well, when I'm wrong, I'm wrong.

"Think fast, Dana!" Anne screamed from behind me. I threw myself to the ground just in time. She heaved two eggs at once. They both whirred over my head and dropped onto the grass with a sickening *crack*.

"Stop it! Stop it!" I heard Brandy shrieking desperately. "It's my birthday! Stop it! It's my birthday!"

Thunk! Somebody hit Brandy in the chest with an egg.

Wild laughter rang out. Sticky yellow puddles covered the back lawn.

I raised my eyes to Anne. She was grinning back at me, about to let me have it again.

Time for action. I reached into my basket and pulled out the one and only egg I had picked up.

I raised it high above my head. Started to throw — but stopped.

The egg.

I lowered it and stared at it.

Stared hard at it.

Something was wrong with the egg.

Something was terribly wrong.

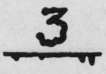

The egg was too big. Bigger than a normal egg. About the size of a softball.

I held it carefully, studying it. The color wasn't right either. It wasn't egg-colored. That creamy off-white. And it wasn't brown.

The egg was pale green. I raised it to the sunlight to make sure I was seeing correctly.

Yes. Green.

And what were those thick cracks up and down the shell?

I ran my pointer finger over the dark, jagged lines.

No. Not cracks. Some kind of veins. Blue-and-purple veins crisscrossing the green eggshell.

"Weird!" I muttered out loud.

Brandy's friends were shouting and shrieking. Eggs were flying all around me. An egg splattered over my sneakers. The yellow yolk oozed over my laces.

But I didn't care.

I rolled the strange egg over and over slowly between my hands. I brought it close to my face and squinted hard at the blue-and-purple veins.

"Ooh." I let out a low cry when I felt it pulsing. The veins throbbed. I could feel a steady beat. *Thud. Thud. Thud.*

"Oh wow. *It's alive!*" I cried.

What had I found? It was totally weird. I couldn't wait to get it to my worktable and examine it.

But first I had to show it to Anne.

"Anne! Hey — Anne!" I called and started jogging toward her, holding the egg high in both hands.

I was staring at the egg. So I didn't see Stubby, her big sheepdog, run in front of me.

"Whooooa!"

I let out a cry as I fell over the dog.

And landed with a sickening crunch on top of my egg.

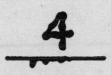

4

I jumped up quickly. Stubby started to lick my face. That dog has the *worst* breath!

I shoved him away and bent down to examine my egg.

"Hey!" I cried out in amazement. The egg wasn't broken. I picked it up carefully and rolled it in my hands.

Not a crack.

What a tough shell! I thought. My chest had landed on top of the egg. Pushed it into the ground. But the shell hadn't broken.

I wrapped my hands around the big egg as if soothing it.

I could feel the blue-and-purple veins pulsing.

Is something inside getting ready to hatch? I wondered. What kind of bird was inside it? Not a chicken, I knew. This was definitely not a hen's egg.

Splat!

Another egg smacked the side of the garage.

Kids were wrestling in the runny puddles of yolk on the grass. I turned in time to see a boy crack an egg over another boy's head.

"Stop it! Stop it!"

Brandy was screaming at the top of her lungs, trying to stop the egg fight before every single egg was smashed. I turned and saw Mom and Dad running across the yard.

"Hey, Anne — !" I called. I climbed to my feet, holding the weird egg carefully. Anne was frantically tossing eggs at three girls. The girls were bombarding her. Three to one — but Anne wasn't retreating.

"Anne — check this out!" I called, hurrying over to her. "You won't believe this egg!"

I stepped up beside her and held the egg out to her.

"No! Wait — !" I cried.

Too late.

Anne grabbed my egg and heaved it at the three girls.

5

"No — stop!" I wailed.

As I stared in horror, one of the three girls caught the egg in midair — and tossed it back.

I dove for it, making a headfirst slide. And grabbed the egg in one hand before it hit the gravel.

Was it broken?

No.

This shell must be made of steel! I told myself. I pulled myself to my feet, gripping the egg carefully. To my surprise, it felt hot. Burning hot.

"Whoa!" I nearly dropped it.

Throb. Throb. Throb.

It pulsed rapidly. I could feel the veins beating against my fingers.

I wanted to show the egg to Mom and Dad. But they were busy breaking up the egg fight.

Dad's face was bright red. He was shouting at Brandy and pointing to the yellow stains up and down the side of the garage.

Mom was trying to calm down two girls who were crying. They had egg yolk stuck to their hair and all over their clothes. They even had it stuck to their eyebrows. I guess that's why they were crying.

Behind them Stubby was having a feast. He was running around in circles, lapping up egg after egg from the grass, his bushy tail wagging like crazy.

What a party!

I decided to take my weird egg inside. I wanted to study it later. Maybe I'd break off a tiny piece of shell and look at it under the microscope. Then I'd make a tiny hole in the shell and try to see inside.

Throb. Throb.

The veins pounded against my hand. The egg still felt hot.

It might be a turtle egg, I decided. I walked carefully to the house, cradling it in both hands.

One morning last fall Anne found a big box turtle on the curb in front of her house. She carried it into her backyard and called me over. She knew I'd want to study it.

It was a pretty big turtle. About the size of a lunch box. Anne and I wondered how it got to her curb.

Up in my room I had a book about turtles. I knew the book would help me identify it. I hurried home to get the book. But Mom wouldn't let me go back out. I had to stay inside and have lunch.

When I got back to Anne's backyard, the turtle had vanished. I guess it wandered away.

Turtles can be pretty fast when they want to be.

As I carried my treasure into the house, I thought it might be a turtle egg. But why was it so hot? And why did it have those yucky veins all over it?

Eggs don't have veins — do they?

I hid the egg in my dresser drawer. I surrounded it with my balled-up socks to protect it. Then I closed the drawer slowly, carefully, and returned to the backyard.

Brandy's guests were all leaving as I stepped outside. They were covered in sticky eggs. They didn't look too happy.

Brandy didn't look too happy, either. Dad was busy shouting at her, angrily waving his arms, pointing to the gloppy egg stains all over the lawn.

"Why did you let this happen?" he screamed at her. "Why didn't you stop it?"

"I tried!" Brandy wailed. "I tried to stop it!"

"We'll have to have the garage painted," Mom murmured, shaking her head. "How will we ever mow the lawn?"

"This was the worst party I ever had!" Brandy cried. She bent down and pulled chunks of eggshell from her sneaker laces. Then she glared up at Mom. "It's all *your* fault!"

"Huh?" Mom gasped. "My fault?"

"You didn't hard-boil the eggs," Brandy accused. "So it's all your fault."

Mom started to protest — but bit her lip instead.

Brandy stood up and tossed the bits of eggshell to the ground. She flashed Mom her best dimpled smile. "Next year for my birthday, can we have a Make-Your-Own Ice-Cream Sundae party?"

That evening I wanted to study my weird green egg. But we had to go visit Grandma Evelyn and Grandpa Harry and take them out to dinner. They always make a big fuss about Brandy's birthday.

First, Brandy had to open her presents. Grandma Evelyn bought her a pair of pink fuzzy slippers that Brandy will never wear. She'll probably give them to Stubby as chew toys.

Brandy opened the biggest box next. She pulled out a pair of pink and white pajamas. Brandy made a big fuss about them and said she really needed pajamas. She did a pretty good acting job.

But how excited can you get over pajamas?

Her last present was a twenty-five-dollar gift certificate to the CD store at the mall. Nice present. "I'll go with you to make sure you don't pick out anything lame," I offered.

Brandy pretended she didn't hear me.

She gave our grandparents big hugs. Brandy is a big hugger. Then we all went out for dinner at the new Italian restaurant on the corner.

What did we talk about at dinner? Brandy's wild birthday party. When we told Grandma and Grandpa about the egg fight, they laughed and laughed.

It wasn't so funny in the afternoon. But a few hours later at dinner, we all had to admit it was pretty funny. Even Dad managed a smile or two.

I kept thinking about the egg in my dresser drawer. When we got back home, would I find a baby turtle on my socks?

Dinner stretched on and on. Grandpa Harry told all of his funny golfing stories. He tells them every time we visit. We always laugh anyway.

We didn't return home till really late. Brandy fell asleep in the car. And I could barely keep my eyes open.

I slunk up to my room and changed into pajamas. Then, with a loud yawn, I turned off the light. I knew I'd fall asleep the moment my head hit the pillow.

I fluffed my pillow the way I liked it. Then I slid into bed and pulled the quilt up to my chin.

I started to settle my head on the pillow when I heard the sound.

Thump. Thump. Thump.

Steady like a heartbeat. Only louder.

Much louder.

THUMP. THUMP. THUMP.

So loud, I could hear the dresser drawers rattling.

I sat straight up. Wide awake now, I stared through the darkness to my dresser.

THUMP. THUMP. THUMP.

I turned and lowered my feet to the floor.

Should I open the dresser drawer?

I sat in the darkness, trembling with excitement. With fear.

Listening to the steady thud.

Should I open the drawer and check it out?

Or should I run as far away as I could?

GET
Goosebumps®
by R.L. Stine

Scare me, thrill me, mail me GOOSEBUMPS now!

Available wherever you buy books, or use this order form. Scholastic Inc., P.O. Box 7502, 2931 East McCarty Street, Jefferson City, MO 65102

Please send me the books I have checked above. I am enclosing $_____ (please add $2.00 to cover shipping and handling). Send check or money order — no cash or C.O.D.s please.

Name _____ Age _____

Address _____

City _____ State/Zip _____

Please allow four to six weeks for delivery. Offer good in the U.S. only. Sorry, mail orders are not available to residents of Canada. Prices subject to change.